PANTS
ON
FIRE

J. M. JOSEPH

HODDER CHILDREN'S BOOKS

First published in Great Britain in 2021 by Hodder & Stoughton

1 3 5 7 9 10 8 6 4 2

Illustrations by Samuel Perrett

A CIP catalogue record for this book is available from the British Library.

ISBN 978 1 444 95470 8

Typeset in Sabon by Avon DataSet Ltd, Arden Court, Alcester, Warwickshire

Printed and bound by in Great Britain by Clays Ltd, Elcograf S.p.A.

The paper and board used in this book are made from wood from responsible sources.

Hodder Children's Books
An imprint of Hachette Children's Group
Part of Hodder and Stoughton
Carmelite House
50 Victoria Embankment
London EC4Y 0DZ

An Hachette UK Company

www.hachette.co.uk
www.hachettechildrens.co.uk

FOR BETH

PART ONE

a quiz ☑

1. A theatre producer flies to London to see you. He claims he will take you to America and make you the MOST FAMOUS CIRCUS STAR IN THE WORLD. Do you:

A) Hop wildly about the room and shout, 'YES! YES! YES!'?
Or
B) Decline, explaining that you must stay in school because your education is more important?

If you have answered A, proceed to the next question.
If you have answered B, stop pretending. We both know the correct answer is A.

2. Before you leave London, a MI5 agent visits. He warns you that a shape-shifting SUPERVILLAIN is at

large and poses a threat to you and your friends. Do you:

A) Ignore his advice? SUPERVILLAINS exist only in Bond films and comic books. Why worry?
Or
B) Cancel the trip to America? It's better to be safe than sorry, especially if your friends are involved.

If you have answered A, proceed to the last question. If you have answered B . . . are you mad? Pass up an all-expenses-paid, three-month holiday of a lifetime in New York? The correct answer is A.

3. While in New York, you discover that the RICHEST MAN IN THE WORLD plans to clone the Ancient Incan potion which gave you superpowers and use it to live forever! Do you:

A) Panic, run about madly in circles and plunge head first into trouble?
Or

B) Overcome your fears and work together with your mates to make the world a better place – whatever the cost?

Surprise! Both A and B are right. You can't go wrong on this one!

My name is Aidan Sweeney – yes, FIRE BOY himself – and I'm back! So buckle up, friend, and take a deep breath before you turn the page. My latest sizzling adventure is here and it is red-hot!

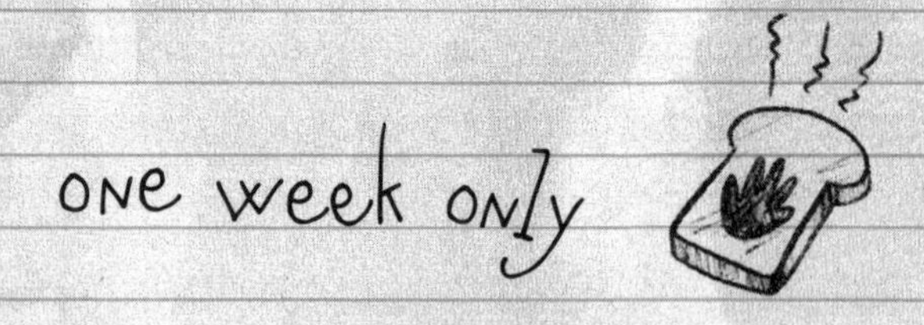

Mist covered the circus grounds. A cold wind rattled the door and drizzle smeared the round windowpane above my bed. The caravan creaked, its old oak panels and slatted ceiling moaning in the pale daylight.

Did I mention it was a Monday morning?

A wet Monday morning?

In November?

Ugh.

I crawled back under the bedsheets. Three or four blissful minutes passed before my absence was noted.

'AIDAN!' Mum shouted.

I poked my head out from under the sheets. At the foot of the bed, Lemon stretched her paws. Her tail flicked once.

'Come on,' I said, rising slowly and swinging my

feet on to the floor. 'Let's get some breakfast.'

Lemon, it seemed, had other ideas. Rolling on to her side, she closed her eyes.

'Go on. Rub it in,' I said, turning my back on her.

I slouched into the kitchen.

Alone.

'Good morning!' Mum beamed, throwing her arm around me. 'I was wondering when you'd show your face.'

'Morning,' I grunted, nose buried in the folds of her bathrobe. 'Have you been up long?'

'Ages!' Mum said.

I believed her.

Mum was a morning person. Waking at dawn for a run or pottering about the house at sunrise was 'fun'.

Madness, if you ask me.

If I were Prime Minister, bed-rest until noon would be mandatory, one of the central planks of my government and a certain vote-winner. More pyjama time – that's the way forward.

I broke free of her grasp and opened the cupboard.

Removing a slice of bread from its packet, I placed it between my palms. As my hands became red-hot, the bread sizzled and browned.

'I wish you'd use the grill for that,' Mum tutted.

'Toast tastes better hand-flamed,' I said, 'Crispy, golden-brown and ready to eat in five seconds. You can't beat that.' Assuming I didn't incinerate it, that is. You can go through a loaf of bread in no time hand-toasting it, if you're not careful.

Mum handed me a plate. 'Try not to drop crumbs wherever you go.'

As I bit into the crust, Mum expanded on the evil of crumbs (which were, according to her, a welcome mat for mice). An update on her never-ending battle against Dirt and Grime followed.

The war was not going well.

Dirt and Grime were advancing steadily on the floorboards (filthy); infiltrating the curtains (in need of a wash) and had overrun the toilet (disgusting).

I ate my toast in silence.

Contradicting Mum by suggesting that the caravan looked fine was not an option. I had gone down that road in the past and it did not end well. I knew my place. I was, at best, a lukewarm ally in her struggle against Dirt and Grime – not much help and often accused of being in league with the enemy. My job wasn't to protest. My role was to applaud Mum's efforts.

So I did.

Toast finished, I tried to sneak back into bed for a quick lie-down before school. Mum, however, was alert to this tactic, so I was forced to retreat to the loo for some 'alone-time'. Afterwards, I dressed swiftly and, were it not for a missing shoe, might have been on time. While Mum waited at the door with her bike, I conducted a frantic search while carefully avoiding the back bedroom where my grandmother (aka 'Granny' or 'the She-Bear') was still asleep.

The shoe, I discovered, was wedged under the sofa.

A last goodbye nuzzle with Lemon and I was ready.

Outside, the mist was thinning. Though the drizzle had stopped, the sky remained a milky-grey. The caravan park seemed eerie in the morning light – no performers outside, no music, no noise or laughter.

Beyond the fence, the Big Top was dark too. The maroon-and-gold striped canvas remained shrouded in the mist, its bunting limp and wet. Shorn of their neon glow, the stalls – the Wild West Shooting Gallery, the Whack-a-Mole, Hook-a-Duck and the Wheel of Fortune – appeared drab. No organ music piped. The shuttered carousel didn't turn.

At the gate, I undid the padlock.

Mum glanced at the sign high above us. 'I'm going to miss walking past the Big Top each morning.'

The sign said:

ONE WEEK ONLY!

ZARATHUSTRA'S
TRAVELLING CIRCUS

The World's Greatest Travelling Circus

featuring the FLYING FLAMING SENSATION . . .

FIRE BOY!

Underneath, there was a gigantic photo of Fire Boy (me) soaring over the circus tent. A trail of yellow flames flickered behind me as I blazed across a blue sky.

I opened the gate.

Pointing her bike south, Mum lifted herself up on to its pedals. 'I ought to be back before tonight's show.'

She blew me a kiss.

I waved goodbye.

Mum eased down the path. By the time she hit the road, she was cycling hard.

I closed the gate.

One more week!

I still couldn't get my head around it. In seven days, Zarathustra's Travelling Circus would leave London and head north. In a week's time, they'd be in Manchester, and Glasgow two weeks later. By Christmas, they'd be in Dublin.

And where would I be?

Right here in London.

It didn't matter how long the queues for Fire Boy were or how famous I'd become. Without Mum's permission, I was going nowhere – and she wanted me to stay in school. I had tried *everything* to convince her.

I had begged.

I had sulked.

I had used my little boy's voice to coax and moan.

I had sent angry plumes of smoke spiralling out of my ears, nose and mouth.

None of it had worked. Mum wasn't budging.

No circus meant no more caravan.

No more carousel rides and carnival games.

No more Dmitri.

No more Mathilde or Atlas or Krazy Klowns or my other circus friends.

No more Big Top.

No more Fire Boy.

Looping the chain between the rails of the gate, I clamped the padlock shut and took one last long look at the photo of me flying.

What's the point of having a superpower if you can't use it?

light my fire

Hold on, you say. A boy who burns and flies? What kind of nonsense is this?

Reader, I know it sounds far-fetched, but it's true.

I can transform my skin, bones, heart, lungs, hair, toenails – the whole lot – into flames and back again in the blink of an eye. Unlike other human beings, fire cannot harm me. I can gargle with gasoline, blow flames out my nose and fart rings of smoke.

Impossible, you say?

Hardly.

A highly entertaining account explaining how I acquired my fiery powers already exists. Penned by yours truly, Aidan Sweeney, it goes by the name of *FIRE BOY* and is available at all good bookstores. Do buy yourself a copy and remember that all profits go to a worthwhile charity – ME. Until then, a helpful guide for new readers and a reminder for old friends on how I became FIRE BOY follows. It should bring everyone up to speed on recent events in Sweeney-land.

The origins of my flame-tastic powers

Six weeks ago, a parcel arrived in the post with my name on it. Inside was a jar of handmade minty sweets called Nature's Own, made in the cloud forests of Peru.

Nice, eh?

You don't know the half of it.

Hidden inside each sweet was a capsule containing a drop of fruit juice from *el Árbol de los Dioses* (the Tree of the Gods), the sacred tree of the Ancient Incas. Legend has it that fruit from this fabled tree unleashes god-like powers in whoever tastes it.

(Spoiler alert: I tasted it.)

But how did this magical fruit juice get inside a package of sweets addressed to me?

Good question. To answer *that* we need to travel halfway around the world, and another six months back in time, to when an environmental scientist at Cambio Laboratories named Sloane Sixsmith went hiking near the Ancient Incan stronghold of Machu Picchu in Peru. At the base of a cliff, she spotted an odd little tree. Knots of silvery branches sprouted from its bone-white trunk. Crowning this tangle of twigs was a single green-skinned berry held aloft like a ring on a royal cushion. The curious Sloane decided this strange tree required further study. She took cuttings from its trunk and branches and placed them in the sealed envelopes, which – like the good environmental scientist she was – she always carried with her. The following day Sloane returned to her office at Cambio Laboratories and placed these samples under a microscope. What did she find? Only that this tiny tree resembled NO OTHER LIVING ORGANISM ON THIS PLANET! Its molecular structure was out-of-this-world!

Cambio Laboratories wasted no time safeguarding their remarkable find. They replanted the tree inside their greenhouse and installed a protective perimeter around it. They erected a high fence and hired armed guards. No one was going to nick their discovery!

Staff at Cambio clamoured to see this remarkable tree. Could it be the legendary *Árbol de los Dioses*? Might its single green-skinned berry grant SUPERPOWERS to whoever tasted it?

Most employees at Cambio Laboratories were like Sloane: inquisitive scientists eager to know more about the origins of *el Árbol de los Dioses*.

Others saw an opportunity. For them, this odd little tree was a ticket to fame, wealth and power.

Enter Ash Aitkens.

A former British Army lieutenant, Ash Aitkens was the managing director of AA Security. Cambio Laboratories had hired his firm to install CCTV cameras in and around its greenhouse. Aitkens soon heard the rumours about the tiny tree which they kept locked inside. He plotted to steal its fruit by targeting poor, innocent Sloane Sixsmith. Aitkens befriended the lonely scientist and the two soon became inseparable. Aitkens even told Sloane (feel free to look away now, the rest of this sentence is only for those of you with a strong stomach) that he loved her.

I know.

Yuck.

Worst of all, Aitkens didn't mean it. On the *very* day Sloane engineered a way to turn the tree's green-skinned fruit into a serum, he betrayed her. Aitkens set off an explosion inside Cambio's greenhouse which destroyed the tree and severely injured Sloane. The ten capsules of fruit serum, however, were safe. Smuggled out of South America in a jar of sweets, they were already winging their way across the ocean . . .

It was a clever idea. By posting the jar of sweets to a

schoolboy in London, Aitkens avoided suspicion. If you haven't already guessed (c'mon, keep up at the back!), that schoolboy was me.

My address wasn't plucked at random. Aitkens had served alongside my dad in the Army. He knew my father had died in an automobile accident and planned on taking advantage of it. Shortly after the sweets were posted, he rang my mum, telling her a parcel was on its way, containing a souvenir my father had wanted me to have. Aitkens begged my mum not to open it until he arrived in London. He intended to swap packages when he got there – giving me a music box he nicked years ago from my dad, while he walked off with the jar of sweets.

Unfortunately for Aitkens, he never got the chance.

I opened the parcel as soon as it arrived.

Inside, I found the jar of Nature's Own (yes, the very one mentioned at the beginning of this section), containing ten minty sweets dusted with sugar and laced with liquorice.

Yum.

I ate one. So did my mates, Sadie and Hussein, each of us biting through the jelly coating and puncturing the capsule of serum hidden inside.

Not so yum.

Almost immediately, our bodies underwent incredible changes.

I could burst into flames and fly.

Sadie could move objects – tennis balls, chairs, people – around the room just by thinking about them.

Hussein could mind-meld with machines. Computers or engines would do whatever he wanted, whenever, as long as he was in physical contact with them.

Once our powers developed, we had many INCREDIBLE adventures – I joined the circus; Sadie disarmed a gang of thugs; Hussein drove a clown car – and, more importantly, we managed to defeat Ash Aitkens in the end (though not before he swallowed TWO capsules and found himself transformed into a long-tailed, super-quick man-monkey!).

So, there you have it – my superpowers explained. No radioactive spider bites or exploding planets! Just a bit of science, a legendary Ancient Incan tree and a jar of sweets I was never supposed to open.

Now let's get back to *this* story. When we left off, I was on my way to school. I know, hardly promising, but don't worry. It gets better.

Secondary schools in London come in all sizes. Some are modern, purpose-built buildings with high ceilings, open-plan settings and state-of-the-art science labs. Some are run-down and in need of a lick of paint, better IT, larger classrooms and more resources.

And then there's Caversham.

An excerpt from *A History of Caversham School*:
Caversham School, a mixed comprehensive for 11-18 year olds in the London borough of Camden, has a colourful past. Formerly known as Flaystreet Prison, Caversham once housed London's most notorious villains. Its thick grey-stone walls and tall iron gate are a reminder of this infamous past. When Flaystreet closed in the 1980s, the Council voted to turn the former penitentiary into

a secondary school. Out went the locks and shackles, in came desks and chairs. Walk around Caversham School today and it is hard to believe that its modern classrooms were once prison cells.

Hard to believe?

Think again.

Ruts in the stonework remain from the bars that once sealed each window shut. Rolls of barbed wire are still rooted to the high walls surrounding the grounds, a barricade littered with punctured footballs and plastic shopping bags blown there by the wind. As for housing London's most notorious villains, take a peek inside the Sixth Form block – if you dare – where you'll find Camden's most promising gangsters learning their trade.

It was a ten-minute stroll from the circus grounds to the school gates. Skirting past a herd of 5th formers who were loitering outside the main buildings, I went in search of Hussein. I found him at our usual haunt, outside the railings near D Block. Sneaking up from behind, I blew a gust of steam down his collar.

Hussein shot into the air like he had stepped on hot sand.

Hah!

He hadn't wriggled his hips like that since last summer's End-of-Year Disco.

Laughing at Hussein, however, caused a lapse of concentration which I soon regretted. Guard down, I accepted Hussein's handshake when offered and fell for the old batteries-hidden-in-the-blazer-pocket trick. Redirecting the batteries' charge with his electro-powers, Hussein zapped me with a bolt of electricity.

Yowza.

If you had stuck my nose into a socket at that moment, I could have lit up Piccadilly Circus on my own. Smoke trickled out of one ear, my hair stood on end and I had to stuff my hand into my mouth to stop the tingling. For some reason, Hussein found this amusing. He fell to the ground laughing.

While I smouldered, a crowd formed around me and Hussein (who was giggling like a deranged hyena). It was led by the King Rat himself, my fellow classmate and sworn enemy, Mitchell Mulch.

'Well, what do we have here?' Mulch mocked.

'Aziz and Sweeney – Caversham's very own Itchy and Scratchy!'

Hussein's grin faded.

I removed my hand from my mouth with as much dignity as I could muster and turned to face my nemesis.

Mulch and his gang – a bunch of mean-spirited lemmings impressed by the money Mulch flashed and the car his father drove – advanced. 'I don't know whether you two clowns have noticed,' he sneered, 'but we're not in nursery school any more.'

The lemmings jeered.

Did I want to point a flaming finger at Mulch and tell him to buzz off?

Yes, I most certainly did.

Unfortunately, such a course of action was not allowed. Messing about with Hussein with no one around was one thing, but there it stopped. Drawing attention to one's superpowers in public was off-limits, *especially* with a blabbermouth like Mulch nearby.

Rule #1 from *The BIG BOOK of Superheroes*:
A secret identity is vital to the wellbeing of a superhero's family and friends. Safeguard it at all costs!

If I used my flames on Mulch, the whole world would soon learn I was Fire Boy. Most people believed my powers were an illusion, that Fire Boy was a circus act who fooled the audience into believing he could burn and fly. I intended to keep it that way, though that didn't mean I had to back down.

'Isn't there somewhere else you ought to be, Mulch?' I snapped.

'As a matter of fact, Sweeney, there IS somewhere I will be flying off to soon. First class, of course, somewhere VERY special,' Mulch crowed. 'But that's a secret not worth sharing with the likes of *you*.'

Before I could spell out to Mulch how little I cared, the first bell sounded.

All round Caversham, from the furthest reaches of its bike shed to the inner sanctum of its staff-room, a mighty groan could be heard. It was the start of another school day.

Hussein and I bundled through the doors of D Block. Mulch, his minions and the rest of our English class followed closely behind.

Miss Spatchcock was waiting.

Miss Spatchcock watched us slouch in, ticking our names off the register as we found our seats.

Four phrases (in no particular order) that best describe Miss Spatchcock:

- A newly qualified teacher, i.e. young, enthusiastic and still fond (for now) of children
- Pale, slim, bespectacled; a champion of creative writing, live theatre and graphic novels; fond of inspirational mottos and/or life stories
- Vastly superior to her older colleagues (most of whom struggle to find the 'on' switch) in all matters involving the use of phones, iPads, smartboards, etc. for educational purposes
- Quite possibly the only person in Caversham School (including staff, students, groundsman,

etc.) wearing a smile this Monday morning

Miss Spatchcock pressed the palms of her hands together. 'I am so looking forward to this morning's lesson! Today marks the start of our new topic on reporting the news. It's a project I *know* you will all enjoy!' Miss Spatchcock chirruped.

I gazed around the room.

Three of the lads in the back row were yawning. The other two had closed their eyes.

In the middle of the room, Freddie Reynolds struggled to undo the zipper of his overcoat.

Four students were staring out the window at cloud formations. Some stared blankly at the board.

Isabella Fink pointed at Freddie Reynolds and mouthed a comment to the two girls next to her.

From her seat in the front row, Maria Vialli raised her hand.

'Miss! Miss!' she cried. 'I knew we were doing newspapers next so I brought some in to share. Should I get them out?'

Those children who were not asleep, studying the sky or tugging on the zipper of their overcoat, turned slowly towards Vialli.

The room became noticeably chillier.

'There's always one,' Hussein hissed, leaning in.

This was a bit rich coming from Hussein, who sucked up to teachers whenever he could. I let it pass without comment, however. Until I was sure how much charge was left in those batteries in his pocket, I wasn't taking any chances.

'How thoughtful of you, Maria!' lauded Miss Spatchcock, adding a wink that left Vialli red-faced and clucking in her seat.

On my left, Hussein scowled. It sounded like he was grinding his teeth.

Recharged batteries or not, winding him up was too hard to resist. 'Weren't you thinking about bringing in newspapers too?' I asked him.

'I was,' Hussein huffed. 'But somebody,' he said, laying great stress on the word *somebody*, 'told me not to bother.'

I shook my head. 'You missed a trick there, mate.'

He glared at me.

'Come on, Hussein. Give credit where it's due.' I pretended to applaud Maria. 'Good to see someone puts in a bit of effort around here.'

'*Shut up*,' he snapped.

The overhead lights dimmed and the two of us – like everyone else in the class – stopped speaking. Images of headlines, newspapers and TV ads whizzed past as Miss Spatchcock's smartboard sparked into life. Photos of politicians, sports stars, floods, beaches and celebrities flew by.

'Twenty-four hours a day, seven days a week,' Miss Spatchcock said. 'The news never stops. Day in, day out, year-round. Information, stories, weather reports, film reviews, football scores.'

The lights came back on.

'Why do some stories make the front page while others get ignored?' Miss Spatchcock asked. She paused, dramatically. 'What makes a story newsworthy?'

Up shot Vialli's hand.

'Something that's current, informative or relevant to society,' she said. 'Examples include live reports from protest marches or battlefronts; public debates on health, the economy and education; and regular updates on global concerns such as climate change.'

'Rubbish,' Mitchell Mulch sneered. 'It's not

what the story is *about* that matters. It's which stories *sell.*'

Joe Jackson agreed. 'Mulch is right, Miss. It's a business. There is no right or wrong. If people buy a paper because it has a dog on a surfboard on its front cover, that story is newsworthy.'

'A dog on a surfboard?' Freddie Reynolds said. 'I'd like to see that.'

'Me too! PLEASE, Miss!' begged Isabella Fink. 'Find us a video!'

Soon a rousing, Fink-led chant of 'YouTube! YouTube!' had everyone banging their desks.

Miss Spatchcock responded swiftly. 'If you can find a story you consider newsworthy in the newspapers I hand out, we can watch a video of *The World's Best Surfing Dogs* before the bell rings.'

Cheers greeted her offer.

'Any story, Miss?' Joe Jackson asked.

'Any story, Joe,' Miss Spatchcock replied. 'In groups of two, I want you to pick out ONE newsworthy item that interests you and your partner.'

There were a few questions.

Jackson asked if he could choose something from the sports section.

Maria Vialli wanted to know if she should make notes on the newspaper itself and highlight passages.

Freddie Reynolds asked if he could go to the loo.

Miss Spatchcock handed out a wad of newspapers. Hussein and I split our sections into two, spreading them out across our table. Flipping through the pages, I scanned the headlines for articles worth reading.

PROTESTERS DEMAND ACTION ON CLIMATE CHANGE

A contender.

DINOSAUR FOSSIL FOUND IN LONDON UNDERGROUND

Like it.

BANK OF ENGLAND PREDICTS INTEREST RATES TO RISE

No way.

CHEESE BEFORE BED DOESN'T CAUSE NIGHTMARES

Interesting.

CACTUS PLANTS TROUBLE BATHERS AT NUDIST BEACH

'You can stop searching, Hussein,' I said. 'I've found our story.'

He didn't answer, too busy reading an article in the bottom corner of his section. Peeking over his shoulder, I scanned its headline.

THEATRE PRODUCER TELLS CIRCUS: 'I WANT FIRE BOY!'

'Gimme that!' I cried, snatching the paper away from him.

TELLS CIRCUS: WANT FIRE BOY!'

The American theatre producer Max Goldman is jetting into London this week with plans to lure Zarathustra's Travelling Circus and its daredevil flying sensation, Fire Boy, to Broadway.

'America is where Fire Boy belongs,' Goldman told reporters. 'New Yorkers will go crazy for him! Who doesn't want to see a kid who can burn and fly?'

Goldman, the producer behind Broadway successes like Pizza: The Musical and When I'm Not Crying, I'm Singing, believes Zarathustra's Travelling Circus and Fire Boy could be his biggest hit yet. 'I guarantee you, people will walk over hot coals to see this show. Fire Boy and Zarathustra's Travelling Circus will be the hottest ticket in town!'

Negotiations between Goldman and Dmitri Medvedev, the ringmaster and proprietor of Zarathustra's Travelling Circus, are scheduled for later this week. So far, Goldman has refused to comment on who the mysterious financial backers for this production are. In a related story, Zarathustra's refuses to confirm or deny rumours that Fire Boy will not be joining them for the remainder of their tour of Britain and Ireland.

Negotiations?

No one had mentioned America to me!

Then again, Mum had been acting strangely lately. When she wasn't stepping outside to take a call, she was checking her messages. Could she—

'Aidan!' Hussein hissed under his breath. He ripped the sheet away from me and smothered it with his sleeves.

I had burnt a hand-sized hole through the newspaper.

The Master of Mayhem

The rest of the morning passed by in a blur.

I couldn't string three words together in English.

Nothing added up in maths.

I hadn't a prayer in RS and in PE I scored twice – both of them own goals.

True, no one seemed to notice. At Caversham, sleepwalking through a school day was a common occurrence.

At least I had Hussein to fall back on.

Arriving early in the canteen, I found us two seats at the end table. Though dangerously close to the Sixth Formers, we were a safe distance from Big-Ears Mulch and the nosy Isabella Fink. Here, we could talk in private.

I shook my head ruefully. 'I wasn't expecting this.'

'Me neither,' Hussein said. 'New York is so far away.'

'I meant *this*,' I said, pointing at the squat brown spud on my plate, moored in a pool of baked beans. A knife slice down its middle revealed two waxy-white halves which looked suspiciously underdone. 'Monday is macaroni and cheese. Baked potato is Tuesday's lunch.'

Hussein pushed his tray aside.

His chin drooped. Worry lines furrowed his forehead and it looked like he was locked in a who-will-blink-first duel with his spoon. *Come on, mate!* I felt like shouting. *Missing out on the mac and cheese is a blow, but there's no need to mope about it.*

Or could there be another explanation for Hussein's gloom and doom?

Might my secret-bearer and comrade-in-arms be *against* me jetting off to America?

I chewed my undercooked potato and considered why.

The answer was in front of me, right here in all its chair-scraping, ear-busting, cabbage-stinking glory.

The canteen.

Caversham's lunch hall was a square pit with a kitchen on one side and hordes of students in groups of two or three or more battling for a place at the long rows of tables. A canteen – or a classroom and playground, for that matter – can be a lonely place when you're sat on your own, and that's exactly where Hussein would be if I left for New York.

I pushed thoughts of Broadway aside and talked footie and gaming. Hussein brightened and lunch sped past. I tried the same trick in the afternoon, parking my circus daydreams at the door and muddling through science. Before I knew it, the final bell had rung.

Boys and girls piled out of Caversham's main doors, storming down the steps and out the school gate. Hussein and I followed, parting at the High Street. He headed north to Alexandria Apartments and I marched west towards Hampstead Heath and the circus grounds.

It was a short trek across two playing fields, past a thicket of spruce trees, up one hill and down another and then there it was: Zarathustra's Travelling Circus.

The maroon-and-gold striped Big Top glowed in the autumn sunlight. Bunting flapped and spun in the breeze and the flag over the circus tent rippled.

And the smells!

Buttered popcorn.

Roasted chestnuts.

The sweet tang of candy floss.

Each afternoon, two of the crew set up stands outside the circus gates and sold nibbles until they were gone. As soon as school was out, children and their parents queued, racing to grab their bag of goodies. The food stands were Dmitri's idea. 'I want children to smile when they think of Zarathustra's,' he told us. Already this afternoon the line stretched to the street. I waved hello to Gareth the magician and Grandpa Yang, the leader of the Red Arrows, who were manning the stalls as I passed by and waltzed through the gate.

Inside the grounds, Atlas was grunting through a workout, slinging two giant dumbbells left and right. Dead-Eye was hosing down her Wild West Shooting Gallery, spraying water at its rows of ducks and bull's eye targets.

Near the entrance to the Big Top, stood the carousel. Its waterproof canvas cover had been removed and left folded on the ground. The carousel's rides – glossy black ponies, tall dragons and long-tailed mermaids – shimmered in the cold November sunlight as if to beckon children forward. I spied three crouched figures aboard the carousel – Dmitri, Mathilde and . . .

'Sadie?' I cried.

'Aidan!' she shouted. 'Come in here! You've got to see this!'

I ran forward.

Sadie was my oldest friend. Seeing her was a treat these days. Unlike Hussein and me, she didn't go to Caversham, so now that Mum and I lived in a circus caravan rather than at Alexandria Apartments I only saw Sadie at Zarathustra's.

I found her knee-deep inside the barrel of the carousel next to Dmitri. What an odd pair the two of them made! Sadie, tall and slender, had on her Lady Pandora's school uniform. Dmitri, a stocky bear of a man, was kitted out in a paint-splattered blue boiler suit. Behind them, in ripped denims and a T-shirt was Mathilde, Zarathustra's young fortune-teller. Arms folded, she was slouched in a carousel bench, her legs draped over the mane of a smiling zebra.

'Oh, good,' Mathilde said. 'Zee Master of Mayhem has returned.'

A short note on the 'Master of Mayhem':

Before I fly into the Big Top, Dmitri warns the crowd that Fire Boy is also known as:

1) The Schemin' Demon: a devilish prankster who plays tricks on friends and foes
2) The Hot Prince of Beel-ze-bub: an imp imprisoned for thousands of years beneath the pyramids of Egypt for being a naughty boy
3) The Master of Mayhem: a flaming demon who has returned to the Land of the Living but cannot be trusted

I ignored her and hopped on to the platform.

The panels concealing the carousel's centre had been removed, exposing the organ's bellows, pipes and the rotating clockwork gears that turned it. Bent over its crankshaft, Dmitri held his torch and pliers like a surgeon as he poked around inside.

Sadie pulled me nearer and pointed to the revolving cogs. 'When the weights and springs inside move, the organ plays. It's a musical clockwork.'

'The only way you will interest him in zat organ is if you throw petrol over it and burn it,' Mathilde snorted.

'Don't give the boy ideas,' Dmitri chuckled. 'I am fond of this old carousel.'

'Now that you mention it,' I said, slapping the rump of a silvery wooden unicorn, 'this ride would burn quickly.'

'You're becoming obsessed, Aidan,' Sadie said, laughing. 'You know he can't even pass a barbecue or grill without stopping to stare at their flames,' she told Mathilde.

'Or bonfires,' Mathilde smirked. 'He is fond of zem too, I believe.'

Sadie and I both froze.

Mathilde gave Sadie a sly grin. 'Yes, I read about Bonfire Night at your school last week in the newspaper. Very strange, what happened, wasn't it?'

'*Very*,' Sadie said, fluttering her eyelashes innocently at Mathilde.

Every year on the 5th of November, the children, staff and parents of Lady Pandora's School for Girls gather on the manicured lawns outside Pandora House to celebrate Bonfire Night. A giant bonfire is assembled and a straw Guy Fawkes tossed on to its centre. Later, after the bonfire has been lit, fireworks are launched and steaming mugs of hot chocolate handed round. Everyone goes home happy.

Until this year.

BONFIRE MADNESS!

STAMPEDE AT LADY PANDORA'S WITNESSES CLAIM 'GUY' RISES FROM FLAMES AND WALKS

Lady Pandora's School for Girls is still reeling after last night's mystifying Bonfire Night celebrations. Numerous reports allege that a burning figure rose from the pyre when the bonfire was lit and spoke to the crowd.

Alarmed, the crowd of schoolgirls and their parents rampaged through the grounds, trampling Lady Pandora's prized rose garden and causing untold damage to the school's croquet lawn.

At first, witnesses claimed, nothing had seemed out of the ordinary. In line with school tradition on Bonfire Night, the founder of Lady Pandora's School for Girls, Lady Arabella Pandora, arrived in a horse-drawn carriage holding aloft the school's famed lightning rod to shouts of 'Huzzah!' from the crowd. An all-girl choir sang 'Jerusalem' as Lady Pandora descended from her carriage and walked over to the wood pile on the South Lawn.

On top sat the 'Guy' tied to a stake. As is the custom at Lady Pandora's on Bonfire Night, the straw dummy had been dressed in the green and black knickerbockers of Sir Reginald Manning's School for Boys, a local rival. Lady Pandora spoke briefly about the Gunpowder Plot and how we remember it each year by burning an effigy of Guy Fawkes. Then, brandishing her lightning rod, she lit the bonfire.

As the 'Guy' burst into flames, Lady Pandora and the crowd again shouted 'Huzzah!'.

And then, observers claim, the burning Guy stood.

'Flames burst from its head and arms,' Portia Wainscott, a student at Lady Pandora's, told the *Hampstead Gazette*. 'He began to walk down the wood pile towards us, and everyone started screaming. When the barriers around the fire crumbled and flew off, we turned and ran.'

Yes, that was me in the green and black knickerbockers on top of the wood pile – and how pleased was I to burn *that* kit off.

The flying barriers?

Sadie.

She whisked them aside with her telekinetic powers. To the crowd, it looked like a mighty sorcerer – me – had flung the barriers aside and was marching towards them, ready to send them to their doom. No wonder they ran.

Hussein was there too. He rejigged the public address system so that it played a haunting tune as soon as I started walking down the wood pile. For the crowd gathered around the bonfire, it must have felt like they were extras on the set of a horror flick.

Were Lady Pandora and her schoolgirls frightened by this strange turn of events?

Reader, we terrified them.

Newspapers claimed the next day that their screams were heard as far away as the Cliffs of Dover. My ears were still ringing two days later.

Was it worth the effort?

Absolutely.

Bonfire Night at Lady Pandora's is a *legend* now. Epic. The stuff of tall tales and rumours. Everyone had an explanation for the flaming Guy who had stood and walked: it was a flaming branch that only resembled a person; Sir Reginald Manning and his schoolboys had played a cunning prank on their rivals; Guido Fawkes had come back to life; and many more.

Whose idea was it?

That, my friend, I am not allowed to say. I am not a snitch nor ever will be, but ask yourself this: which of us – Sadie, Hussein or me – knew the grounds of Pandora House, its school traditions *and* the timings? Who among us laughed the hardest at seeing Lady Pandora legging it up the lawn for all she was worth?

I shall say no more.

Back at the carousel, it seemed like a convenient time to move the conversation away from Lady Pandora's. I wanted to talk about New York, not fright night and fireworks.

'Speaking of newspapers, I saw an article at school today. It said a theatre producer wanted to take Zarathustra's to New York. *With* Fire Boy. Is this true?'

'That would be brilliant!' Sadie squealed.

Dmitri removed his head from the inside of the organ. He glanced at Mathilde, then me.

'Yes,' he said at last. 'What you read is true. The Americans want to talk to us. They are interested in the circus – and especially Fire Boy.'

'Dmitri!' Sadie cried. 'You *must* go! New York is incredible!'

Dmitri nodded his head while Sadie quizzed him about where they would stay and what they would do in New York.

I listened, but said nothing.

It's hard to explain what I felt. Sure, I was buzzing at the thought that I could carry on as Fire Boy. And yes, I very definitely wanted to travel to America. But it seemed best not to get my hopes up. If Mum had said no to Manchester, it didn't seem likely that she would agree to me crossing an ocean.

Dmitri pulled a rag out of his back pocket and wiped the grease off his hands. 'Come,' he said to me, patting the dolphin bench opposite Mathilde. 'Sit. We talk.'

Sadie and I squeezed into the carousel bench.

'Two days ago, I get call from America. This producer wants a circus now. Not in six months. Not in a year. *Now*. This I do not like. It is not how you run business. Plus, when I think about America,' he winced, rubbing his knee, 'I get ache.'

I stared at him. 'Thinking about America hurts your leg?'

'He means zis offer gives him bad feeling,' Mathilde explained. 'When Dmitri's knee aches, it is warning.'

'Or it means I am getting old,' Dmitri said with a wink. 'So, I say nothing about offer to anyone.'

'Only to me,' Mathilde said.

Dmitri nodded. 'Only to Mathilde.' He rubbed his knee and frowned. 'My leg tells me to carry on. My leg says keep to tour dates and go to Manchester.' Bowing his head, the ringmaster sighed. 'But my heart? It tells me to go to America. Go to New York because, if we do, there is better chance my young friend and his mother will stay in circus. New York means opportunity. History – the first circus on Broadway – and that, I want. We *all* want. Aidan is one of us now, his mother too, though she does not want to admit it. Circus blood. Zarathustra's is family and family stays together.'

Family.

Dmitri and Zarathustra's wanted me to stay with them.

I burnt with pride.

Literally.

Flames flickered from my head and hands as Sadie jumped out of the way – her Lady Pandora's uniform may have been posh, but it wasn't fireproof.

My fire flared for a moment, then died. Though Dmitri's words warmed my heart, I doubted they would have the same effect on Mum.

'Do not worry about your mother,' Mathilde piped up, as if (not for the first time) she were reading my mind. 'She will agree to New York.

My heart leapt like a kangaroo on a trampoline. 'She will?'

'*Oui*,' Mathilde replied.

'You seem very sure of yourself,' Sadie said curtly.

'I am French,' Mathilde sniffed, sitting astride the zebra. 'I am always sure.'

Dmitri put a hand up to shush us. 'For now,

we wait, yes? Nothing is agreed. I must speak with the Americans and if they like circus they must make offer.'

I remembered the article I read earlier. It said a theatre producer, Max Goldman, was on his way. 'What should we do until they come?'

'For now, I suggest you find zee mad old woman before she causes trouble,' Mathilde said.

Mad old woman?

That could only be one person.

Granny!

'What has she done now?' I asked, not entirely sure I wanted to hear the answer.

'Your grandmother has taken zee little cat for a walk,' Mathilde said.

'Lemon?'

But that didn't make sense. Lemon never went for walks. Unless . . . 'No!' I shouted. 'She wouldn't!' Not even Granny would stoop that low!

'Zink again,' Mathilde smirked.

I jumped off the carousel and hit the ground running. 'Come on, Sadie!' I cried, darting towards the Heath. 'We've got to stop her!'

granny returns

I stood on the edge of a gloomy wood. Peering into the glade, I stepped over a knot of brambles and entered. Burrs clung to the legs of my trousers. Thorns picked at my sleeves and still I strode on.

I was a man on a mission.

Ducking under the low-lying branch of a hawthorn tree, I came to a halt. A sprawling clump of briars stood in our way.

'I think we took a wrong turn,' I said.

Sadie scowled at the bush cutting us off. 'Remind me again why we must pick our way through the undergrowth and not take the path like everyone else.'

'Warfare is the art of deception,' I said grimly. 'When faced with a cruel and cunning enemy, a surprise attack is essential.'

'Perhaps,' Sadie said, 'but there is no way I am

crawling under that.' After checking left and right to ensure no one could see us, she flicked her finger. Like a soldier saluting his commanding officer, the briar bush stood to attention, its long branches shooting straight into the air and clearing our path.

'Come on,' Sadie said, walking past it.

I followed her, glancing backwards in time to see the branches fall back into place, resuming their blockade across the windy trail. 'Maybe you should go first,' I said to Sadie.

'Fine,' she replied, stepping over a log.

Our destination was an ancient sycamore. It grew on the edge of a raised clearing that looked over a meadow. A winding path led up to it and a metal bench stood nearby, often used by visitors to the Heath who came to feed the pigeons that gathered in the green.

Reaching the tree, we bent our heads round its knobbly trunk and peeked out.

Got you!

There, on the edge of the meadow, was our target.

Her back was broad, her arms powerful. Her legs rose out of the ground like two great tree trunks. A single bristly eyebrow framed two dark eyes, one wide and glaring, the other a squint. A crown of steel-grey hair, fashioned in the shape of a helmet, adorned her large, bucket-shaped head. In one hand she held a cat carrier, in the other a walking stick, which she swished menacingly through the November night like a pirate's cutlass.

Granny.

For two glorious weeks at the circus, our caravan had been Granny-free. The bliss of not listening to her complain, snore, berate or fart in the evenings! The joys of lying in bed in the mornings undisturbed, unprovoked and unpunished!

Oh, what I would do to have those days back.

Disaster had struck when Granny, in an attempt to distil her own gin, blew the roof off the camper-van Dmitri had lent her. *Kaboom!* How she got hold of a Make-Your-Own-Moonshine kit is anyone's guess, but it left me and Mum with a warning from the police, a van that needed replacing and a miserable, moody, old witch of a house guest in *our* caravan.

And now she had Lemon!

Hidden by the thick tree trunk, Sadie and I

watched as Granny ascended the path towards us. Two dog walkers in tweed jackets and spotless green wellies trooped up the hill behind her. One was short and round, the other lean. They seemed to be chatting. At their feet a small pack of hounds yipped and yapped, bounding through the meadow.

Granny stopped swirling her stick. Planting it into the grass, she smirked. An evil grin snaked across her crooked mouth. She placed the cat carrier on the ground.

Sadie gasped. 'No! She would never.'

'Think again,' I said bitterly. 'This is Granny we're talking about.'

In the meadow, the hounds stopped yapping. Their long noses pointed up and sniffed the air.

'What is it, Millicent?' The short man said. 'Caught a scent, have you, Maude?'

'Hope it's not another squirrel,' the tall man drawled.

'Bad luck for the squirrel if it is,' the short one chuckled.

The hounds shot towards Granny, gathering round her feet. Teeth bared, they snarled at the carrier.

The two dog walkers hurried after them. 'Careful, madam. Beware of those dogs!' the short man panted.

Granny bent down and shook the carrier. 'It seems your pups want to say hello to my grandson's cat.' Grinning at the snapping hounds, she said in a sing-song voice, 'Do the cute little doggies want to play with Lemon?'

'A CAT?' cried the short man. 'Are you crazy?'

'Don't open that, whatever you do!' The tall one shouted. 'Those hounds will tear that cat limb from limb!'

Granny opened the carrier. Lemon's head peeked out.

Four wild-eyed hounds sprang forwards, jaws open. As they leapt into the air, Lemon – a sleepy, six-year-old ginger cat fond of sardines, belly rubs and naps – began to grow. Her body stretched. Her fur thickened and her limbs lengthened. In an eye-blink, Lemon the cat was gone and in her place was a tiger, three metres long and weighing around 250 kilos.

The cat carrier was shattered to bits.

ROAR! growled Lemon.

Whimper, whimper, whined the hounds, scrabbling backwards and spraying wee left and right. Spinning round, the terrified dogs raced down the slopes, ears bent and tails tucked under them.

'HELP!' cried the dog walkers, dashing after their hounds as swiftly as their legs could take them.

'Ho! Ho! Ho!' cackled Granny. Shaking with laughter, she hooted and hollered as Lemon chased the men and their dogs round the meadow.

An impossible sequence of events, you say?

I'm afraid not, reader.

Like Sadie, Hussein and me, Lemon too had swallowed a sweet with a drop of fruit juice from *el Árbol de los Dioses* inside it. And now, it seemed, Granny was using my cat's powers for her own twisted ends.

The old witch! Granny had crossed the line, leaving me with no choice. I had to hit her where it hurt.

Indignant, I marched towards her. 'We saw that!' I cried as Sadie emerged from the woods behind me. 'You can't use Lemon like that! Something could happen to her!' It was time to unleash the deadliest weapon at my disposal.

Pointing a fiery finger at her I cried, 'I'M TELLING MUM ON YOU!'

Did Granny hang her head in shame?

Did a pang of remorse flit across her craggy features?

Did she at least say she was *sorry*?

No, no and no again.

'Tattle-tale!' Granny sneered, flicking her stick at me and missing me by a whisker. 'Go on. Run to your mother! See if I care! If the cat means that much to you, go fetch her yourselves! I'm off to the pub.'

And, without another word, she stomped off leaving Sadie and me to corral a tiger.

Lemon ambled leisurely after the four hounds and their masters, stretching her long, powerful limbs. The dogs fled, yipping and yapping and racing at full throttle through the tall grass. Their masters followed, though they found this pace hard going. Red-cheeked, eyes white with fear and lips an alarming blue, the shorter man seemed in dire need of a lie-down. His taller partner was not faring much better. Though faster, he kept stopping to wheeze and pound his chest while throwing frightened glances back at the tiger prancing after them.

Granny, meanwhile, had tramped off to find the nearest bar stool.

A short note about Granny:

In most children's stories, grannies fall into two categories. The first kind are smiley old women with white hair and round glasses. They bake cookies. They cook roast dinners. They knit scarves which are too long and their hands flutter joyfully when a baby is near.

The second kind are 'cool' grannies. These ladies haven't yet twigged that they are old. They drive fast cars. They wear suits, skirts, tracksuits, beads, feathery hats, rings on each finger and leopard print, often all at the same time. They are loud. They allow grandchildren to eat what they want, when they want, and they take your side when you ask your parents if you can stay up late.

There is, however, another category.

Most stories for children – being fond of prancing unicorns, rainbow-filled skies and happy endings – prefer to avoid these grannies. Because this kind fart and belch. These grannies guzzle gin and scratch their bottoms in public. They root for villains and laugh when children fall over and scrape their knees. In their hands, hairpins and walking sticks are weapons, useful tools to prod and trip passers-by.

My granny falls into this category.

'Lemon!' I called. 'Come here, girl!'

Sadie clapped her hands, I whistled, but it was no use. Lemon ignored us.

I tried once more, this time with an offer she might find too enticing to resist. 'SARDINES!' I bellowed at the top of my lungs. 'WHO IS GOING TO HELP ME EAT THESE YUMMY SARDINES?'

In the meadow, Lemon halted mid-prance. Her magnificent orange, white and black-striped head turned. Her whiskers twitched.

I pulled the tin out of my trouser pocket – one I kept tucked away in case of tiger emergencies such as this – and waved it over my head.

Her amber eyes blinked.

Flicking her long tail, Lemon spurned the fleeing hounds and their masters and padded across the meadow in search of worthier prey.

Fish.

A short note about Lemon:

Not long after consuming the minty Nature's Own sweet with its hidden capsule, Lemon discovered she had the ability to transform into a fully grown tiger. As you may have guessed from her un-tiger-like interest in sardines, Lemon remains a cat inside a tiger's body. There was NO chance of her taking a bite out of either those hounds or their walkers. In fact, if the hounds had tried to chase *her* back, chances are that Lemon would have scooted up a tree.

Marvellous, you say. A tiger for a pet – you must be over the moon!

I am.

But there are drawbacks. If a tiger decides to sun herself on the sofa, you had better find another seat because there is no shifting her. A tiger can claw open a refrigerator; break a bed when she hops on to it; stare you down rather easily when it comes to begging for food. And as for what a tiger leaves behind in her litter tray . . . let's not even go there.

Thank goodness we had Dmitri on hand. Long before Dmitri became ringmaster of Zarathustra's Travelling Circus, he was an animal trainer. He showed us how to train Lemon (never easy to do with any animal, let alone cats) to transform on command. All it takes now for Lemon to change from cat to tiger or back again is to nuzzle her under the ear and say 'Pushkin' at the same time.

We keep Lemon as a cat most of the time. We could never afford to feed a tiger (a fully grown tiger can consume up to thirty kilos of meat in one day) or allow one to roam freely the way Lemon does. And, as we saw with the dog walkers, a tiger puts the wind up people (and hounds) pretty fast.

Lemon slunk nearer, eyeing the sardines hungrily. 'Good girl,' I said, beckoning her forwards.

'She's so beautiful,' Sadie trilled. 'Look at how her flanks shimmer.'

I got down on one knee (though now, as a tiger, Lemon's head towered over me). She looked like she could swallow the sardine tin and my arm in one go. 'Come a little closer.'

Lemon nudged forwards. She rubbed the side of her head against my chest.

I clung on to her neck, pushed backwards by her force, and scratched the soft fur under her chin and behind her ear. 'Pushkin,' I whispered.

A moment later, a ginger cat with white markings and a hint of black fur materialised.

I opened the tin of sardines.

Lemon placed her paw on the lid and went to work.

Sadie joined me on the ground, running her hand over Lemon's shoulders and hind legs. 'She is the world's most amazing cat. Her elasticity alone is incredible. A biochemist would sell their soul to get Lemon under the microscope—'

'Not that it would ever happen,' I interrupted. 'Not while I'm alive.'

'Not that it would ever happen,' Sadie continued, 'but the way her muscles, bones and fur expand and shrink in an instant is miraculous.'

As Lemon nibbled at the sardines, a police officer came running towards us. 'You children must evacuate the Heath immediately!' she ordered. 'There are reports that a tiger has escaped from the zoo. We cannot take any chances!'

'*Another* tiger?' I said under my breath to Sadie. 'What are the chances of that?'

Sadie rolled her eyes. '*Not* another one, Aidan.' She nodded her head at Lemon.

Oh.

I glanced down. After licking the tin clean, my cat was now curled around my foot.

Meow, said Lemon.

It was beginning to get dark on the Heath. A runner struggled uphill, red-faced and sweating. Two commuters walked home, one carrying a briefcase, the other chatting into his phone.

Sadie, Lemon and I hadn't budged. We were still being questioned.

PC Odiah lowered her notebook. 'Let me get this straight. People think your *cat* is a tiger?'

'It happens a lot,' I said.

A stony-faced PC Odiah stared at me. '*This* cat?' she asked, pointing her pen at Lemon.

The three of us bowed our heads and watched Lemon weave between us, rubbing against our legs and purring.

'She's much fiercer than she looks,' said Sadie.

'A killer,' I added. 'You wouldn't want to meet her alone in a dark alley.'

Lemon yawned. Flopping on to the soft grass, she stretched her limbs. Her eyes closed.

'Right,' PC Odiah said. She shut her notebook.

'You should have seen her a few minutes ago,' Sadie said. 'She was racing around the place, wasn't she?'

'Like a beast,' I said.

'You wouldn't know it was the same cat,' Sadie said.

'If you say so.' As PC Odiah slid her notebook and pen into her jacket pocket, her radio buzzed. Turning away from us, she held it to her ear.

'I don't think she believes our story.'

'I guess you can't blame her.' Sadie said, picking up Lemon and cradling her into her chest. 'She must think we're mad.'

True.

It's not as if we had much of a choice. If we told PC Odiah the truth and revealed Lemon's secret, the police would show up at my caravan door and cart her away. They would tell me that they had no choice: a tiger-cat was a threat to public safety. They would lock Lemon away in a cage and we might never see her again.

Not a good option.

But if we said nothing at all, we ran the risk of allowing police, zookeepers, helicopters and reporters to hunt for a tiger which, technically speaking, didn't exist. Sadie and I didn't want that either.

PC Odiah swung round. 'Every tiger in England's zoos and safari parks are accounted for,' she said. Seeing Lemon draped over Sadie's forearm, her stern expression softened. 'Is she asleep?'

'Stalking prey is hard work,' I said.

'So I hear,' PC Odiah said. She stuck a finger out and tickled Lemon under the chin. Lemon arched her neck and purred.

Straightening her bowler hat, PC Odiah zipped up her high-visibility jacket and scanned the shadows stretching over the woodlands. 'This is the third time this week I've been called out to hunt down a tiger.'

Sadie and I exchanged glances.

I ought to string Granny up and slow-roast her over a pit.

'People ring in telling us they've spotted a tiger on the Heath chasing pigeons. Pigeons! Can you believe it?'

Yes, I could, as a matter of fact.

'What's next?' PC Odiah ranted. 'Flying saucers landing on Kenwood House? Water dragons in the Thames?' Narrowing her eyes, she regarded me closely. 'Mind you, I haven't forgotten the last time we met in the Big Top. You don't ever forget seeing . . . a man . . . like that, do you?'

No, you don't.

That 'man' she was referring to was Ash Aitkens – a six-foot man-monkey covered in fur and sporting a tail – a sight one tended to remember.

'Still, I'll be sorry to see the circus leave,' PC Odiah sighed.

This was more like it.

Nothing put a fizz in my step more than hearing people rave about Zarathustra's. Whenever anyone mentioned how much they enjoyed seeing Fire Boy under the Big Top, my insides blazed like a four-alarm-fire (in other words, I like it).

'Are you a fan of Fire Boy, officer?' I asked, struggling to keep a straight face. 'I hear he's brilliant.'

'A fan of Fire Boy?' PC Odiah scowled. 'Hardly! How they let that fire hazard walk around, I'll never know. I will miss the overtime though. Big crowds mean extra shifts.' PC Odiah tapped the brim of her hat once and walked off. 'Keep safe,' she called over her shoulder, 'and stay away from tigers.'

I waited until PC Odiah was some way off then said sourly, 'There's no pleasing some people.'

Sadie laughed. 'You should speak to my mum. There are no in-betweens in show business, Aidan. People either hate you or adore you.'

'I prefer the adorers.'

'Too much attention isn't good either,' said Sadie. She flicked the broken handle of Lemon's carrier with the end of her shoe. 'What are you going to do with this?'

There wasn't much left of it. Its lid was torn, the screen was ripped in two and bits were scattered everywhere. Her carrier was never meant to contain a fully grown tiger. 'Looks like I'll have to carry Lemon Tart home myself. Any chance you can help me clear this mess?'

'Sure,' Sadie said.

Up from the grass rose the bits and pieces of the cat carrier, some near our feet, others metres away. Chunks of plastic – the lid, its handle – and bits of metal and cloth drifted up into the air. Gathering into a dark cloud, they buzzed past us and flew swarm-like into a bin at the bottom of the hill.

'You should sing like Mary Poppins when you do that,' I said.

'I prefer to chant. It's more theatrical.' One arm cradling Lemon, Sadie waved her other hand as if casting a spell and began to mutter. As she spoke, the fallen leaves underneath a nearby spruce tree stirred. '*Muddied leaves of mottled brown, forsake your bed upon the ground. Awake! Skywards fly on my command.*'

The leaves climbed higher. Lemon – wide awake now and eyes widening – watched as they began to spiral round the tree. Round and round the leaves flew, a blur of yellows and browns.

Faster and faster they went until – *whoosh!* – Sadie let go. 'This is making me dizzy,' she said.

The leaves fluttered slowly down like giant curly snowflakes. Two passing runners stopped to stare at the sky.

'It's getting late,' I said. 'I ought to go. Dmitri will be wondering where I am.'

Sadie kissed Lemon on the nose and handed her

over. 'Make sure you tell Dmitri what Granny's been doing.'

I promised I would.

'And text me if you hear any more news about New York,' Sadie called as she waved goodbye.

I watched her walk away. When I couldn't see Sadie any more, I made my blazer into a cat-sling – buttoned down the front with my hands cradled round the bottom – and slid Lemon inside. Together we headed back to the circus.

Everyone was talking about Zarathustra's Travelling Circus the next morning. A reporter from the BBC arrived to interview Dmitri. Radio stations mentioned us in their hourly news bulletins. Newspapers put our story on their front pages (bottom corner, but still).

Why was Zarathustra's Travelling Circus suddenly headline news?

Simple.

Delilah Jones was involved.

BILLIONAIRE'S GRANDDAUGHTER SEEKS CIRCUS CURE

What do you give a man who has everything?

The answer, it seems, is a circus.

Yesterday, reports in New York confirmed that Delilah Jones, granddaughter of the billionaire tycoon, Clayton Jones, is behind attempts to install a circus in Central Park.

Clayton Jones is chairman of the multi-media corporation, Frontier, and one of the world's richest men. For decades, Jones has shaped public opinion on both sides of the Atlantic. Presidents and prime ministers alike courted him, knowing that his newspapers and television networks could sway voters.

A sudden illness, however, has forced Jones to withdraw from the public eye. The 64 year old refuses to leave his Fifth Avenue apartment and now oversees his Frontier News and Media empire from his sickbed.

Might a circus compel the ailing billionaire to step outdoors?

His twelve-year-old granddaughter, Delilah, thinks it can.

'My granddaddy

always said that he has three great loves: me, money and the circus,' said Delilah Jones. 'The first two he's got. A day doesn't pass without him seeing me and Lord knows my granddaddy's got enough money. That just leaves the circus. I want to bring a circus here for every New Yorker, not just my family. This old world has gone to hell in a handbasket, you know what I'm saying? A no-holds barred, singing and dancing circus is what I want to see, and so does my granddaddy.'

Delilah Jones is her grandfather's only surviving descendent. Her parents, Rupert and Maisie, died in an open-sea accident outside Brisbane, Australia when Delilah was a baby. The two extreme-sports enthusiasts had hoped to show the world that snorkelling with sharks was good, safe fun. Sadly, they were mistaken. Delilah has lived with her grandfather ever since.

Like her grandfather, Delilah clearly wastes no time when her mind is set. She has enlisted the services of Max Goldman, theatre producer, and tasked him with finding a circus that might bring a smile to her grandfather's face. To date, Goldman has visited circuses in Oslo, Los Angeles and Brazil in his search for 'the world's best circus'. This week, it is London's turn. Goldman arrives on Thursday, and he will be sitting ringside when the curtain lifts at Zarathustra's Travelling Circus.

Zarathustra's Travelling Circus is a traditional, family-owned circus run by its ringmaster, Dmitri Medvedev. Star attractions include: Dead-Eye, a sharp-shooter; Mathilde, a young fortune-teller who reads tarot cards; and Atlas, a Greek strongman.

Their most recent addition, the flying sensation, Fire Boy, has helped propel Zarathustra's into the top tier of circuses. Fire Boy's flying act with its fiery somersaults and flaming spins have left audiences spellbound. Since Fire Boy joined its line-up, Zarathustra's has played to sell-out crowds.

Can Fire Boy's flames lure Clayton Jones out of his apartment?

Will Max Goldman give him that chance?

Delilah Jones and the circus-loving public of New York City will learn the answers to those questions shortly.

Underneath the report there was a photo of Delilah at her grandfather's birthday party – there were a gazillion candles on the cake, so I'm assuming it was the old man's bash. Delilah stood next to her billionaire grandfather. She had a heart-shaped face and long copper hair.

Her teeth were so white they sparkled.

A caption added that Delilah read comics and loved spicy foods. 'If it's got Tabasco sauce sprinkled on top, I'll eat it,' she said.

Interesting.

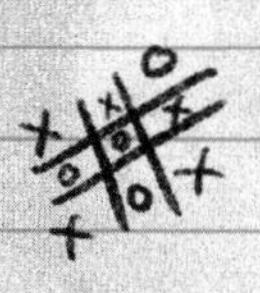

wednesday

Nothing much happened.

I was backstage in the dressing room when my phone buzzed.

Everyone – from Dmitri to little Zhang Li (the youngest of Zarathustra's gymnastic troupe, the Red Arrows) – froze.

'It's Hussein,' I said.

There was a giant intake of breath.

They all knew Hussein was my lookout man. Armed with a pair of binoculars and a giant box of popcorn, he had agreed to climb into the perch above the Wild West Shooting Gallery and act as sentry until a certain someone showed up.

A text message sent from Hussein Aziz to Aidan Sweeney at 7:10pm:

A gold limo is approaching the entrance.

'A gold limo just pulled up!' I cried to the room.

The rope-walker, Kenise Williams, clasped her hands together in prayer.

Atlas grunted.

Gareth the magician closed his eyes and crossed his fingers.

I stared at my phone and waited.

The

Tension

Was

Unbearable.

My phone buzzed again.

A text message sent from Hussein Aziz to Aidan Sweeney at 7:12pm:

The Eagle has landed. Repeat. The Eagle has landed.

'HE'S HERE!' I shouted. 'HE'S HERE! MAX GOLDMAN IS IN THE BUILDING!'

Inside the dressing room, it was pandemonium.

'Yeehaw!' cried Dead-Eye Dolores, shooting her six-gun into the air (the one with blanks, luckily).

The Red Arrows clapped their hands in harmony.

Eshe and Rodrigo danced.

Gladys the Wonder Dog howled.

The Kerrigan brothers in their Krazy Klowns costumes hugged each other while the seated Mathilde shrugged, scissoring one leg over another.

'I told you zee American would come,' she said.

As the first bars of our entrance song began to boom over the loudspeakers, Dmitri gathered us into a huddle.

'My friends,' Dmitri said, his voice thick with emotion. 'Ten, twenty years ago, Zarathustra's travelled the world. Everywhere children came to see us. And then . . . it stopped.'

Dmitri's blue eyes clouded. 'A trip to the circus lost its magic. Crowds dwindled. Children stayed away. You remember those days, don't you? Many nights we went hungry. The circus became smaller and so did we.'

Removing his top hat, Dmitri hung his head and stared at the tips of his ringmaster's boots.

Breathless, we waited – all of us – for him to finish, because there was NO WAY he was leaving it there.

'Until now,' Dmitri said, placing his great paw of

a hand on my head and grinning at me. 'The magic is back. We are great circus. Not good. *Great.*' He cracked his whip in glee.

SNAP!

'Tonight, we show Max Goldman who we are! It is time for Zarathustra's to cross the oceans again, yes?'

'YES!' we shouted.

'Zarathustra's!' Dmitri cried, clenching his fist.

'ZARATHUSTRA'S!' we replied.

I retreated quickly to the ice tub we kept in the corner of the dressing room because I was in danger of exploding into flames.

Useful in emergencies, that.

'You all right, mate?' Shane Kerrigan asked as he stuffed a whoopee cushion, a firecracker and a rubber chicken into the pockets of his clown suit.

I gave him a thumbs up. 'I'm fine,' I said through the steam rising from the tub of ice. 'Never better.'

Two hours later, I stood alone in the dressing room waiting to go on for our encore, the 'Inferno'.

So far, so good.

Tonight's show had been a scorcher. If that

performance hadn't wowed Max Goldman, nothing would.

The Krazy Klowns were on top form. Kenise Williams dazzled on the tight rope. Dead-Eye Delores notched bull's eye after bull's eye. The Red Arrows dazzled. Mathilde astounded. Gareth made Gladys the Wonder Dog disappear and Atlas lifted the Krazy Kar over his head – twice.

And as for yours truly, I cannot be modest.

I was stupendous.

I had blazed through the Big Top as Fire Boy. I had completed – steady yourself, friend, because this might come as a shock – I had completed my first ever error-free routine.

Yes, you read that right.

Error-free.

I hadn't set fire to the circus tent.

There had been no in-flight 'accidents'. I hadn't collided with the centre pole or burnt the trapeze ropes (or the ringmaster stand) when coming in to land.

I hadn't scorched Donal and Shane or set fire to the Krazy Kar.

I had kept my temperature within safety limits

(i.e. no one complained of heat stroke or passed out).

It had been a master class in flying flamboyance, and now all that was left were our final bows.

The rest of the cast were lined up in the wings for their introductions. Me? I had to cool my heels and wait backstage instead.

Alone.

Turning slowly round, I studied my reflection in the full-length mirror on the wall of the dressing room.

Honestly, the state of this costume.

Scorch marks ran down both sides. Holes had burnt through its elbows and knees. My long tail had been so charred that only a curly stump was left. I shook my bottom at the mirror and sighed.

Some demon.

I looked like Peppa Pig with two pine cones glued to her forehead.

Straightening my horns, I tugged my tail and told myself it didn't matter – my flames would hide the holes.

Turning away from the mirror, I checked the live feed. On the monitor, a grinning Dmitri strode into the ring and stood in the spotlight like a circus king in his red ringmaster's coat and top hat.

I had five more minutes.

Being last out for the encore had its advantages. Backstage was usually a madhouse with people rushing in and frantic searches for scarves, swords or magic wands. Now it was empty, apart from me and the left-over rubbish a show produces: mirrored tables covered in cotton balls, eyeliner brushes, tissues, sponges and make-up pots; jars of Vaseline left open on shelves; empty crisp packets on the floor; black tights, scarves and a sparkly jacket tossed over folding chairs; and the scent of hair-spray hanging heavily in the air.

I turned up the volume on the live feed.

'*Please put your hands together for the greatest showmen and women on Earth*,' Dmitri roared into the microphone.

'*First, join me as we welcome back . . . DEAD-EYE!*'

A spotlight fell on the entrance and out ambled Dolores in her black leather coat and cowboy hat. Aiming a six-gun in the air, she fired confetti into the crowd.

Three more minutes.

'THE KRAZY KLOWNS!'

On the monitor screen, the Kerrigan brothers skipped into the ring, tooting their silly horns and blowing kisses.

'ATLAS!'

The giant Greek strongman strode in, flexing his mighty muscles.

'MATHILDE!'

The French teenager in Goth make-up and a fortune-teller's dress strutted forwards, chin high and her dark eyes blazing.

One by one the acts shimmied, somersaulted and pranced into the centre ring. Forming a circle around Dmitri, the circus performers took their spots and waved to the cheering crowd.

'*WAIT!*' Dmitri suddenly cried. '*There is mistake.*' Wheeling around atop his ringmaster's stand, he counted the circus performers. '*One is missing.*' He scrunched his bushy eyebrows and stroked his chin. '*Who might that be?*'

'*FIRE BOY!*' the crowd shouted.

'*Who?*' Dmitri asked.

'*FIRE BOY!*' they screamed more loudly.

'*Fire Boy!*' Dmitri cried, slapping his palm against his forehead. '*Of course! Now where could that little devil be?*' Throwing his head back, he scanned the rafters of the circus tent for me. The performers joined him.

Guess what? I wasn't there.

'*It seems Fire Boy will not be returning this evening*,' Dmitri said sadly. '*Demons cannot be trusted.*' He shrugged. '*What can we do?*'

The crowd groaned.

Dmitri's face fell. '*I am sorry, but—*'

'*WAIT!*' Mathilde cried. '*I see him!*'

The Big Top fell silent as the fortune-teller stepped forwards, her eyes closed as if in a trance and one hand in the air. '*I see a boy of fire over zee rooftops of London.*'

Dmitri hopped off his ringmaster's stand and ran to her. '*Is he headed this way?*'

Mathilde opened her eyes and smirked. ''*Ee is.*'

I strolled towards the curtains that separated backstage from the main tent as Dmitri launched into my opening. '*Cursed for his impudence, imprisoned for centuries, he is free – free at last!*' Dmitri cried. '*Ladies and gentlemen, boys and girls, that naughty devil is back! FIRE BOY HAS RETURNED!'*

I leapt into the air and ignited.

By the time I reached the centre ring, I was at full throttle, spewing flames and burning hard. Below me, the crowd roared. I waved to Sadie and Hussein in the upper deck and swooped over the box seats where Max Goldman sat spellbound with an unlit cigar in one hand and his mouth wide open. After circling the Big Top three times, I finished with a loop-the-loop and a shower of exploding fireballs.

Shielding his face from the heat, Dmitri held the microphone over his head so I could speak into it as I hovered above him.

'BRACE YOURSELVES, LONDON,' growled a deep-throated, pre-recorded voice (me, talking into a Scary Voice Changer app Hussein had downloaded on his phone). 'FIRE BOY IS BACK AND HE IS READY TO BOOGIE.'

Red, orange and blue spotlights spun, transforming the centre ring into a dance floor. A glitter ball covered in mirrored scales descended from the top of the circus tent and the music began to play.

Twisting in mid-air, I shot sprays of flames in time to the beat. Burners located around the centre ring sent jets of fire upwards.

Dmitri wiggled his hips. Atlas flexed. Mathilde pointed a finger skywards.

Eshe and Rodrigo, our trapeze artists, twirled and spun, and we all danced along in time. When the music neared its end, I broke away from the line-dance and whizzed around the Big Top, setting off indoor fireworks. Faster and faster I zoomed, fizzing through the screeching flares and starbursts of sparks as the circus stars danced below me. I halted directly above Dmitri just as the music ended and – *BOOM!* – The Showstopper, a pyrotechnic extravaganza of screaming rockets, fiery showers and shooting stars, exploded.

Now *that's* what I call entertainment!

When the applause died down, we returned to the dressing room.

We were buzzing! Tonight's show had been red-hot!

The Kerrigan brothers tooted their horns.

Dead-Eye whooped.

Kenise Williams sang a few bars of 'Disco Inferno' and Gladys the Wonder Dog wagged her tail.

'It was as if zee crowd did not want us to leave,' Mathilde marvelled as she wiped away her black lipstick with a wet cloth. 'Zey wanted more. More. MORE.'

Dmitri removed his top hat. 'Tonight was good, yes?' he said, raking a hand through his tangle of curly grey hair.

'Magic!' Gareth chirped.

'I could have danced all night,' Eshe sang.

'A personal best,' Atlas grunted, eyeing the outline of his biceps in the mirror.

Donal Kerrigan removed his floppy hat and tossed it on the table. 'Special kudos to the little man in the devil suit.'

'Aye,' Shane said, undoing the laces of his clown shoe. 'The lad from London was on fire.'

'He wasn't the only one,' Finbar, the third Kerrigan brother, sighed, fanning the singed bottom of his red-and-white striped pants.

Everyone laughed.

Fire Boy setting fire to the Krazy Klowns was a crowd-pleaser and one of my favourite parts of the show. How they hopped about and shouted when their trousers were on fire!

Dmitri wrapped his big arm around me. 'You see? *This* is why we join circus. To give people memories. Those people will remember tonight's show for many years.'

'So will I, Dmitri,' I said.

'You are good boy, Aidan,' Dmitri rubbed my shoulder. 'I am lucky man to have you in my circus.'

I tried to speak, but words stuck in my throat.

Nothing came out except steam and smoke.

It was an awkward moment, soon forgotten when the dressing room door suddenly received three loud thumps.

Bang! Bang! Bang!

Through the keyhole, a gravelly voice shouted, 'Dmitri! Open up! It's me, Max Goldman! You and I gotta talk!'

Everyone froze. All of us stared at the door. 'C'mon, Dmitri! I know you're in there,' Goldman wheedled. 'Let me in. You're going to like what I have to say!'

It was as if Goldman had flicked a switch.

Kenise punched the air.

Gladys the Wonder Dog barked.

Eshe and Rodrigo tap-danced on the spot and the three Kerrigan brothers leapt chest-first at each other.

Everyone pogoed or grinned or high-fived – but quietly, of course, so Goldman wouldn't hear us.

And me?

Flames crackled from my hair and ears. I was ready to explode with excitement!

Dmitri cleared his throat and said, 'One minute,

Mr Goldman. I am coming.'

Then he scrunched his eyes and patted the air – his signal for calm. To me he whispered, 'Go. Wait in booth. Be silent. Do not come out until he leaves.'

I did as he commanded, nipping into one of the dressing room's changing booths. I closed the curtain behind me, making sure I left a tiny crack open so I could peek out.

Dmitri unlocked the door and Max Goldman burst in.

'Dmitri!' Goldman cried. 'We meet at last!' He grabbed the ringmaster and shook his hand furiously. 'You and I, my friend, are going to make a lot of money together. What a show!'

A short, stocky man with thinning hair, Max Goldman didn't seem able to stand still. He moved his hands when he spoke. He hopped from foot to foot. He rubbed his hands with glee. Though he wore a dark pinstripe suit with no tie and a white shirt opened at the collar, he seemed right at home among the costumes and glitter. A gold chain hung round his neck and gold rings glinted on each of his fingers. He jingled when he walked, his black eyes flickering as he scoured the room.

Nor was he alone. A young man in a trendy blue suit trailed after Goldman, carrying a giant bouquet of red roses, a magnum of champagne and a box of chocolates three tiers high.

Goldman shook hands. He kissed cheeks. He hugged each member of the circus as Dmitri led him around the room introducing the cast by name. Goldman told everyone how talented they were and addressed them as though they were his best mates. Halfway round he turned to the young man. 'Andrew, look at this cast! We've got a Jamaican acrobat, a Greek muscleman, three Irish clowns and I don't know where the magician is from, but it ain't Brooklyn. It's like the United Nations in here!'

'I can't tell you how happy this makes me,' Andrew said, his face hidden behind fifty long-stemmed roses. 'A diverse work force is a—'

Goldman cut him off. 'Andrew! Why are you carrying that around?' he snapped. 'Put the flowers down and open the champagne! I want to make a toast.'

'Yes, Mr Goldman.'

Andrew planted the bouquet in Gladys the Wonder Dog's water bowl (she was not impressed) and dropped the chocolates on a table. The champagne was next. After opening the bottle with a pop, he splashed champagne into whatever containers he could find – paper cups, tea mugs, pint glasses and one single champagne flute (removed from the pocket of his jacket) – which he filled and handed to Goldman.

'To my new friends – sorry, my new *associates* – because I'm telling you, Dmitri, I am not leaving this town until you promise to come to New York! Three months, that's all I want, and I will turn Zarathustra's into the most famous circus in the world!'

Not wanting to be left out, I opened a water bottle which I had found in the changing booth and silently raised it.

'To Zarathustra's!' Goldman declared, holding his glass of champagne high in the air, 'and wherever fortune may take us!'

'I will drink to zat,' Mathilde said, raising her glass.

'To Zarathustra's!' everyone chimed – me included, in a whisper.

Goldman drained his glass in one go. 'Mmmm,

that's good! Now, where is this crazy kid, Fire Boy? Dmitri, I'm telling you – no word of a lie – when that kid came rocketing in on fire my ol' ticker skipped a beat.' Goldman clutched his heart. 'I couldn't believe my own eyes.'

'You *did* go very pale, sir,' Andrew said.

'It was like watching Peter Pan come to life . . . but on fire,' Goldman marvelled.

'Mr Goldman, sir, with all due respect,' tutted Andrew. 'I don't think that's the most child-friendly way to describe—'

Goldman stopped him with a grim stare.

Andrew ran a finger over his lips and locked them. 'I am shutting my mouth right now, sir.'

'So, as I was saying, this Fire Boy, Dmitri! He got so close on one fly-over I think he gave me sunburn.' He lowered his head and patted his balding pate. 'Look! A heat rash! So where is the hot head?' Goldman asked, searching the room. 'Is he here?'

'We never allow Fire Boy to meet the public,' Dmitri explained.

'It is part of his mystique,' Mathilde added, topping up her cup with more champagne. 'Zee less people know about him, zee more eager zey are to see him.'

Goldman's face lit up.

'Now that I can understand! Keep your public coming back for more – that's what we want!' Goldman cried. 'And with my help, Dmitri, the whole world is going to be lining up to see you and Fire Boy perform. Together we are going to turn Zarathustra's Travelling Circus into THE GREATEST SHOW ON EARTH!'

Excited?

You bet I was!

I emptied the water bottle over my head – I couldn't reach the ice tub in time – and gloried in the steam rising off me.

I was going to New York! (Assuming I could talk Mum into it . . .)

'No,' Mum said.

She pushed the box of chocolates towards me. 'You have the last one.'

'I don't mind if I do.'

When it comes down to the last chocolate, you need the reflexes of a jackrabbit if Granny is sitting across from you. I moved lightning-fast, snatching it out of the tray before she could get her greedy claws on it. I dangled it over my mouth. 'You're getting slow, Granny. The years are catching up with you.'

Granny glared at me, her face and hands smeared with chocolate – the old witch had gobbled up the entire top tray as soon as I had opened the box. 'Pig!' she grunted.

'Cat-napper,' I snapped. 'You owe me a cat carrier.'

Granny snorted. Eyeing me angrily, she returned to licking the chocolate off her fingers and face. You needed a strong stomach to watch Granny do that and still want to eat, but I would not be deterred; I lowered the last chocolate into my mouth and chewed.

'Yum,' I said, grinning back at her, my teeth covered in chocolate. 'Caramel. My favourite.'

Granny slammed her walking stick down. 'I'm not going to sit here and watch this spoiled pup gloat. I'm going to bed.'

'Goodnight,' I said quickly, before she could change her mind. 'See you tomorrow.'

'Goodnight, Hilda,' Mum said.

Granny stomped off to the other end of the caravan in a strop without looking back.

Result.

I chewed my caramel in peace.

Dmitri gave me the box of chocolates for a) remaining behind the curtain throughout Max Goldman's visit without making a sound and b) not burning the changing booth down when Goldman said we would be working together.

I continued chewing.

You have to hand it to Dmitri. He knows how to keep his cast happy.

'We're in luck,' Mum said, scrolling through her phone. 'I checked my rota. I'm free Friday night.'

I kicked off my shoes and sank back into the sofa. 'Have you ever been to The Swank before?'

Mum laughed. 'The Swank does not cater for people on my salary.' Curling up beside me, she placed her mug on the armrest and opened her novel. 'I *am* looking forward to having a good nose around though. Max Goldman must be very keen on taking us to America if he wants to buy you dinner there.'

Us?

I inhaled, trying to calm myself before my temperature spiked. Now was not the time to combust with excitement. A cool head was needed if I were entering into negotiations with Mum.

'Does that mean you're considering his offer?' I asked casually.

Mum sipped her tea quietly. 'I will go to The Swank and meet Max Goldman. We owe Dmitri and Zarathustra's that much.'

'Did I mention Goldman is offering us a

short-term contract – three months in New York, all expenses paid?'

Mum sighed. 'Once or twice.'

'I would be back in school before Easter. And think of the fun you and I can have in New York City!'

'It *is* tempting, but let's just wait and see for now, Aidan. We don't want to rush into a decision which we'll regret.'

I nodded my head. 'I understand.'

Though indifferent on the outside, inwardly I oozed confidence. *Wait and see* was as good as a yes. Lemon slinked in. She rubbed her back against the leg of the table, then leapt up next to me on the sofa.

'Do you think we can take Lemon with us to The Swank?' I asked.

'No.'

The Swank.

Before he left our dressing room earlier that evening, Max Goldman had insisted that the circus come to dinner at The Swank on Friday night. His treat, he'd said.

The whole circus!

Atlas alone could pack away three steaks and a leg of lamb. Dinner at The Swank for the whole cast would cost thousands!

This invitation came with one catch though. I had to appear in public as Fire Boy for the first time.

Delilah Jones was jetting over from America to meet us – *all* of us. She was footing the bill and, Goldman explained, 'if Delilah says she wants to meet the cast, she meets the cast'. On Friday night, there would be no hiding behind a curtain.

And that was fine by me. It was the least I could do. If it weren't for Delilah Jones, I would be kissing Fire Boy goodbye on Sunday night. I owed her that much.

Dmitri had insisted that Max and Delilah sign a non-disclosure agreement before accepting the invitation, one that prevented them from revealing my identity to Frontier News or anyone else. Dmitri was determined to keep my name out of the papers. Me? I wasn't so bothered. I was happy to meet with Delilah Jones. In fact, I was looking forward to it.

'Did you know you burnt through your socks again?' Mum said, snapping me out of my thoughts.

I checked my feet.

Mum was right. My toes were showing and the edges of my socks were frayed.

'Oops,' I said, shooting a flame out of each toe. 'My bad.'

Mum sighed. 'Please tell me your shoes aren't in the same state.'

I glanced at my trainers, which were lying next to the door. No holes, but the tips had melted. 'Max Goldman told us that if Zarathustra's moved to New York City, he would be our own little genie. "You rub a lamp," he said, "and – poof! – out I come, ready to make your wish come true".'

'You're going to ask Max Goldman to get you socks and shoes?' Mum asked.

'I might.'

Max Goldman, my very own genie.

I liked the sound of that.

'Mum,' I said, 'If you had one wish, what would you wish for?'

'For starters, something to wear tomorrow night,' Mum said without looking up. 'How about you?'

'Don't know. More wishes, I guess.' Placing my hands behind my head, I wiggled my toes and watched their flames flicker. 'Though you could say Delilah Jones and Max Goldman have granted my wish already.'

'Have they?' Mum said. She put her book down. 'What wish was that?'

'To stay with the circus.' My toe-flames flared suddenly, then disappeared. 'If we go to New York, I can carry on being Fire Boy.'

Fridays at Caversham meant fish and chips, PE in the sports hall after lunch and a gentle wind-down during the day for students and teachers alike as, at last, the weekend beckoned.

Unfortunately, no one had told Miss Spatchcock.

It was Day Five of her *Read All About It* topic. So far, Miss Spatchcock had explained why, despite protests, *The Beano* could not – strictly speaking – be classified a newspaper; discussed the art of headline writing and revealed to us that most people didn't turn to the puzzle pages first when they opened a newspaper. Who would have thought?

Our goal for this term, Miss Spatchcock said, was to compose a newspaper of our own, *The Caversham Chronicle*. 'We are going to compose, edit and publish our very own school newspaper!'

she enthused. 'YOU will be our reporters! YOU will be our editors! YOU will design the layout! YOU will be our publishers!'

Half of the class gaped at Miss Spatchcock in horror. The others continued to stare into space.

There were exceptions.

Maria Vialli bounced joyfully about in her seat, unable to contain her glee.

Isabella Fink groaned, muttering darkly about how unfair it was that Miss Spatchcock's class were expected to produce a newspaper while others weren't.

And then there was me.

A benevolent calm descended upon my features. An inner peace, you might say, the tranquil satisfaction that comes with knowing that this lot would be slaving away writing a newspaper while I swanned off to New York.

Mum permitting, that is.

Back in the classroom, Miss Spatchcock stood behind her desk gauging our reactions. When her gaze fell on me, she blinked. Clearly, my Buddha-like contentment in the face of this avalanche of work had come as a surprise.

‘Aidan,’ she said. ‘Am I mistaken or are you looking forward to writing for the *Chronicle*?’

‘I can’t wait, Miss,’ I said cheerfully. ‘The more assignments, the better. If we are going to publish a newspaper, let’s do it right.’

‘I am so pleased to hear that,’ Miss Spatchcock cooed.

In the seat next to me, Hussein snorted. He knew about Max Goldman, Delilah Jones and New York, of course, and was not fooled by my sudden interest in schoolwork. I flashed him my sunniest smile and received a sour, teeth-grinding stare in return.

My joy increased.

Miss Spatchcock flicked her iPad and a set of instructions for a brainstorming session appeared on the smartboard. She read through each in turn, then asked if there were any questions.

Vialli was first out of the blocks. ‘Will we be expected to know about newspapers for our end-of-year exam?’

When Vialli dropped the e-word, the back row sat up. Like gazelles who had heard a cheetah in the tall grass, their heads lifted. Their blank expressions vanished. Anxious glances were exchanged.

'What?'

'What did she say?'

'*Exam?*'

'There's an exam in English?'

Once startled, this herd was difficult to calm. Miss Spatchcock spent a good five minutes reassuring them that our newspaper project came with no exam attached.

Mulch was up next. He wanted to know who the editor-in-chief of this newspaper would be. Should Miss Spatchcock appoint him – the only candidate with the necessary brains and leadership skills to make it succeed (his words, not mine) – he would agree to take it on. As long as everyone understood they had to answer to him, of course.

That one didn't get far.

Isabella Fink had a question about the newspaper's content. Fink, a keen reader of tabloids and celebrity magazines, asked if she could pen a gossip column for the newspaper. 'Tales from the Girls' Loos' was her suggested title. Fink claimed she had the lowdown on the rest of our year group – proper scandals, by all accounts – and promised to expose all.

The colour drained from Miss Spatchcock's cheeks. 'A gossip column about the other children in your year group would *not* be suitable,' she said.

'But Miss,' Joe Jackson protested, 'if it's *our* newspaper, shouldn't we put in the stories *we* want to read?'

Fink and her mates chimed in with a supporting chorus of 'Please, Miss, please.'

Miss Spatchcock dropped the matey let's-discuss-this mode and ascended the moral high ground. A sermon on how 'a responsible press informs, educates and offers a voice for its citizens' followed. Gossip, rumours, exaggerations and outright lies were a scourge, Miss Spatchcock declared, a blight on modern discourse which we must avoid at all costs.

'So . . . does that mean I can't write a gossip column?' Fink asked.

Miss Spatchcock took a deep breath. 'Isabella, I would sooner pull out my fingernails with rusty pliers than agree to it.'

Ouch.

That sounded like a no to me.

Fink and friends came to the same conclusion.

Wailing in unison, they threw themselves across their desks. 'That is so unfair!' they cried.

I confess that I too was disappointed.

Who fancied who didn't interest me much, but I had hoped Fink would spill the beans about the girls' loos, AKA the Forbidden Zone. Unlike the boys' loos, a cesspit which one entered only out of necessity, the girls' toilets seemed a far more jovial affair. Girls entered (often giggling) in twos or threes. Some entered at the start of break, and stayed there until the bell rang.

Why?

What was its appeal?

Were there lounge chairs in there? A snooker table? Did it resemble a Turkish bath with towels and steam? I mean, the thought of following Hussein into the boys' toilets!

Come on!

Can you imagine? Sharing a bench in the changing room was bad enough.

I had become so distracted by the riddle of the girls' toilets, that I failed to notice the discussion concerning what to put into our newspaper had moved on. When I re-emerged from the kingdom of my mind, I discovered my classmates were intent on interviewing a notoriously publicity-shy circus star.

Me.

Joe Jackson hopped out of his chair as if he had been hit by a thunderbolt. 'I know what this newspaper needs!' he exclaimed. 'Fire Boy!'

Miss Spatchcock's mouth opened and closed. 'Who?'

'Fire Boy. He lights himself on fire and flies through the air! Everyone in London is talking about him and Zarathustra's Travelling Circus,' Jackson cried. 'I've seen him three times.'

A warm glow of satisfaction swelled inside me as I noted how many of my classmates nodded along in agreement. Perhaps I was wrong about Jackson. I had always assumed he was a fast-talking, self-serving backstabber. It seemed that I had underestimated his keen intellect and powers of observation.

'Sweeney's mum handles the A&E for the circus

– he and his mum live on site. She can get us an interview. She must know him!'

Each head in the room swivelled towards me.

'Is this true, Aidan?' Miss Spatchcock asked. 'Does your mother know Fire Boy?'

'They're very close.' I chuckled to myself. 'My mum never tires of seeing him. Great company, Fire Boy. Funny. Clever. Brave. Handsome.'

I paused, momentarily distracted by a groan from Hussein on my left, and carried on. 'And much taller than you'd expect.'

'Whatever you say, Sweeney,' Jackson smirked. 'But I think we should dig up some dirt on this firebug. Investigate who he is and how he makes his fire. The tabloids would pay big money to hear that – we could sell our article to them!'

Perhaps I had been too hasty to reassess Jackson, the swine.

As I launched into a well-rehearsed explanation of why Fire Boy refused to do interviews, there was a knock on our classroom door.

It was Mrs Schwartz, the elderly school secretary. 'Excuse me, Louise. There's a, erm, gentleman here to collect Sweeney and Aziz. He says—'

'Fool! Friend of Fool! It is I, Atlas!' cried Atlas, brushing past Mrs Schwartz. Ducking under the door (so as not to hit his head), he entered sideways (he was too wide to fit otherwise). 'Dmitri requests your presence.'

The class gaped in wonder at the giant Greek strongman. Miss Spatchcock stared first at Atlas, then me. 'Aidan, did he call you . . .'

'Fool? It's a circus thing, Miss,' I nodded. 'Long story.'

Was I worried that Dmitri had summoned me?

No.

It wasn't the first time Dmitri had pulled me out of school. Fire marshals had once insisted on seeing me burning in person before allowing me to perform. Another time, a Danish TV crew showed up unannounced requesting a clip of me flying. True, I didn't usually get to take Hussein with me, but perhaps there was a technical issue at the Big Top. If there was a problem with the sound or lighting, Hussein would have it sorted in no time.

I picked my school bag off the floor and stood. Hussein did the same. 'Can we go, Miss?'

Miss Spatchcock gave us the all-clear, then

turned to Atlas with a smile. 'We were just talking about Zarathustra's when you came in. Am I right in thinking you are a circus performer too?'

'I am Atlas,' he bellowed, ripping his T-shirt in two and flexing his muscles. 'I am the strongest man alive!'

'Oh my!' gasped Mrs Schwartz, glancing up at his bare chest. 'Goodness, I – well, I wasn't expecting that.'

I was.

Give Atlas an excuse to tear his top off, and off it comes. The man goes through three or four shirts a day – and that's not even counting circus performances.

Like a peacock parading in front of thirty young peahens, the bare-chested Atlas flexed his chiselled arms as he strutted round the room.

Poor Miss Spatchcock.

That teacher training college she attended must not have provided tips on best practice when a strongman who loves attention comes for a visit. It seemed as if she didn't know whether to interrupt Atlas or hope for the best and let him carry on. Not that the class minded the interruption. Only

Mulch seemed displeased, arms folded and sulking in his seat.

Ha, ha. Even better.

As Hussein and I moved towards the door, we found Sadie waiting in the hallway.

'Are English classes at Caversham always like this?' she asked, peeking into the room.

I waited for the whoops of applause to die down – Atlas had lifted Miss Spatchcock's massive filing cabinet over his head and was shaking it – before answering. 'Pretty much,' I said. 'What are you doing here?'

'Atlas collected me from Lady Pandora's. He said there's a meeting taking place back at the Big Top and Dmitri wanted me to be there.'

I choked on a mouthful of flames. 'A meeting?'

Sadie's grin disappeared. 'I assumed you'd know what it was about.'

I shook my head. 'Not me.'

'In that case, we had better not waste any time,' Sadie said. 'Shall I hurry Atlas along?'

I looked into the classroom. About ten children were standing on Atlas's back while he did push-ups. He was up to twenty – Mrs Schwartz was leading the counting – and still going strong.

'What did you have in mind?'

'See that pencil under your teacher's desk?' Sadie said. 'Watch.'

The pencil rolled forwards, spinning between the legs of two desks before coming to a stop underneath Atlas. It flipped round on its point so that its rubber was pointing upwards.

'Let's see if Atlas is ticklish,' Sadie grinned, stepping into the doorway for a better view.

Up went the pencil rubber. First it stroked the strongman under his chin, then his armpits.

Vigorously.

Hussein gasped. 'I couldn't do twenty push-ups if I was being tickled.'

'Mate,' I said, 'you couldn't do twenty push-ups full stop.'

Atlas, however, was up to forty before he took much notice, and by that time Sadie had left off the tickling him with the pencil and instead was trying to stick it up one of his nostrils.

He got the hint.

Atlas stopped and lay on the floor so the children standing on his back could disembark. 'Atlas will return and do one hundred push-ups!' he declared, rising to his feet and walking towards us in the doorway of the classroom.

A thunder of applause greeted this announcement, cheers which fell deathly silent when, moments later, the class noticed Sadie standing between me and Hussein.

Sadie Laurel-Hewitt – daughter of a film star and striker for the Arsenal Ladies Under 12s squad – had never stepped foot in Caversham before today. Once again, my classmates' mouths fell open.

'Who's *that*?' Isabella Fink asked, practically frothing at the bit. 'I've never seen *her* before.'

It was the question on everyone's lips, it seemed. And there it remained.

Before I could answer, Atlas tossed Hussein and me over his shoulders and galloped down the hallway. The fleet-footed, long-legged Sadie hurried after us. Whether a piggy-back was what Dmitri had in mind when he asked Atlas to escort us home, I can't say. I could see its advantages though. There was no way Hussein or I could have kept pace with a man-mountain like Atlas. Even Sadie was struggling to keep up and she was fast.

As we cruised up the High Street, I had time to consider who might have called this meeting and why.

It had to be Max Goldman. Nothing else could be this important.

Had reservations for dinner at The Swank fallen through?

Had Delilah Jones and her private jet arrived early?

Had they found a different circus?

No, no and no.

It wasn't Max Goldman who had called us together.

It was MI5.

extraordinary measures

Atlas set Hussein and me down beside the carousel. Due to the jostling we had received aboard his shoulders, the two of us wobbled about like sailors setting foot on dry land after months at sea.

'I think I'm going to be sick,' Hussein moaned.

'Shall I fetch a bucket, friend of Fool?' Atlas asked.

'No,' said Hussein, waving him away. 'Just give me a minute.' He flopped down on to the rim of the carousel.

Still flushed from her run, Sadie examined her shoes. 'I would have worn my trainers if I had known we were going to sprint up the High Street.'

I opened my mouth to complain – I wanted Atlas to explain why we'd had to race here if no one was about – when three black sedans rumbled through the gate.

They parked outside the Big Top.

A very worried Mr and Mrs Aziz stepped out of one sedan.

'Mum?' gasped Hussein.

Mimi, Sadie's stepsister, sprang out of the second, carrying an art folder.

'Mimi?' cried Sadie.

I assumed Mum would hop out of the last car. Instead, a lanky, grey-haired man emerged. 'Aidan,' he said when he saw me. 'We meet again.'

'Hello.'

It was Russell R Whittaker of MI5.

Agent Whittaker and I had first met four weeks ago when the police rang MI5 for assistance. It was Agent Whittaker who had carted Ash Aitkens away after the man-monkey had tried to put an end to Zarathustra's Travelling Circus with a homemade fire-bomb. Agent Whittaker had on the same navy suit and pink tie I had last seen him in, which left me wondering whether this was standard MI5 uniform or the only suit and tie he owned.

Agent Whittaker ushered us inside the Big Top. Mr and Mrs Aziz first wanted to know whether

Hussein was in trouble. Mimi, meanwhile, was angry.

'What's going on?' she huffed. 'One minute I'm walking to work and the next, two MI5 officers stop me!'

'Don't look at me! I haven't done anything!' Sadie cried.

Mimi gathered her stepsister in her arms. 'It's OK, babes. I'm not blaming you. I know it's not your fault.' Looking at me over Sadie's shoulder, Mimi's eyes narrowed into two fierce slits. 'It's you, isn't it?' she asked angrily.

A puff of smoke chimneyed out of my ears.

The possibility that I was responsible for MI5's presence had also crossed my mind. Lowering my head, I walked meekly away until I met Dmitri in the centre-ring He greeted me with a wink, which lifted my spirits. Somebody, at least, was on my side.

'We are all here,' Dmitri said to Agent Whittaker, shaking his hand warmly. To Mr and Mrs Aziz and Mimi, he said, 'Welcome! Please, find seat in bleachers and make yourself at home.'

It was like walking into a school assembly.

In the front row were the very keen – Eshe, Rodrigo, Kenise and Mum (who waved Mimi and

Hussein's parents over). Behind them sat the Red Arrows (in chronological order).

The law enforcement crowd – Granny, Dead-Eye Dolores and Gladys the Wonder Dog – had bagged the corner seats where they could keep a close eye on proceedings.

The too-cool-for-school lot – the Kerrigan brothers and Gareth the magician – talked among themselves at the back.

Atlas couldn't fit into a seat so he was sitting on the steps.

And Mathilde sat opposite Granny, Dead-Eye and Gladys. She wasn't alone though. She had Lemon stretched out across her lap.

Yes, Lemon.

Hussein sat with his mum and dad and Sadie nabbed the seat next to Mimi. Because there were no more empty spots in the front, I joined Mathilde.

I expected Lemon to hop into my lap when she saw me.

She didn't.

Content in Mathilde's arms, Lemon purred like a kitten.

'Your cat often comes to zee caravan to see me,'

Mathilde said, stroking Lemon behind the ears. 'She is fond of me.'

'She gets around,' I said.

Wedging two fingers into his mouth, Dmitri let out a whistle loud enough to wake every dog in a two-mile radius. It was a signal which those of us who worked in Zarathustra's Travelling Circus knew well. It meant: *Shut up and listen.*

The chatter stopped and Agent Whittaker stepped forwards.

Four phrases (in no particular order) that best describe Agent Russell R Whittaker of MI5, age unknown:

- Long-limbed, dark-skinned, brown-eyed, short-haired; sports a goatee flecked with grey hairs
- Gravelly voiced; speaks slowly and in a London accent
- Keen-eyed; prone to intense scrutinies of crime scenes and witnesses which can induce anxiety, sweating and a sudden need to use the loo
- Fond of navy suits and pink ties

'Thank you for coming at such short notice,'

Agent Whittaker began. 'Asking the public to step away from their jobs or pulling children out of classes is a last resort, but in this case, a necessary one. Word reached our offices yesterday evening of a possible threat to your safety. At the moment, it is too early to determine how much danger – if any – the people inside this circus tent are in. However, in this instance, we felt it better to err on the side of caution.'

Agent Whittaker stopped.

Inside the Big Top no one moved or spoke. Everyone held their breath, waiting for him to continue.

'Such extraordinary measures are necessary,' Agent Whittaker said with a steely determination, 'because we are facing a threat unlike any the world has ever seen before . . . and its name is Sloane Sixsmith.'

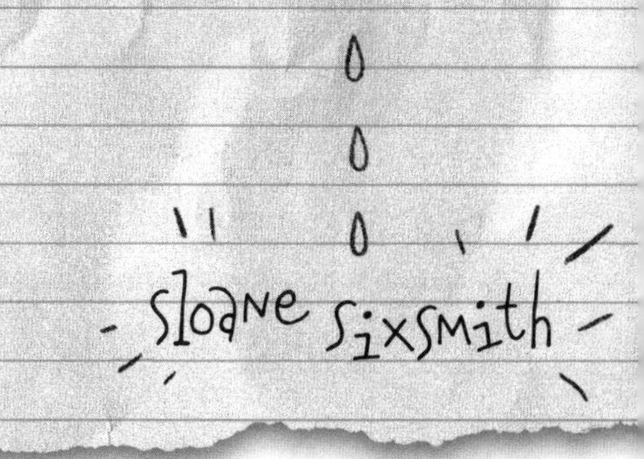

There are a number of ways to respond when told *a threat unlike any the world has ever seen* is slouching towards you. Such as:

The Heroic

Chin high, shoulders square, you throw back your head and laugh. 'Ha! Ha!' you say. 'Let the scoundrel come and I shall send it screaming and crying back to the hellhole from which it came!'

The Calculating

Showing no emotion, you withdraw into the engine room of your mind and begin formulating stratagems, a line of defence and a means of inventing mad contraptions which shall allow you to overcome your foe.

The Cowardly
Your cheeks wobble, your eyes tear up. Throwing yourself to the ground you sob, 'Why me? Why does everyone always pick on *me*?'

For those with the ability to self-ignite (me, basically), there remains a fourth way. You expel smoke from various orifices like a steam engine chugging uphill.

'Stop zat,' Mathilde hissed from the seat next to me. 'Zee Big Top is a no smoking zone. Go outside if you need to puff. You are upsetting zee little cat.'

Draped over Mathilde's knee, Lemon gazed up at me.

Lemon didn't look upset – at least, not compared to others at the ringside. Down there, everyone looked nervous.

Sadie chewed her fingernails.

Sweat seemed to pour off Hussein.

Dmitri slapped his forehead and – I'm guessing here – swore in Russian.

Even the Kerrigan brothers, three hard men who never even winced when slapped on the noggin with a spade or cried when they took a kick in the you-know-where, shifted uneasily in their seats, waiting for Agent Whittaker to tell us more.

Luckily, he did.

'For those of you who have never heard of her before,' Agent Whittaker said, 'it was Sloane Sixsmith who discovered the Tree of the Gods. She came across it while working for Cambio Laboratories in Peru. Because her background was in folklores – the herbs and remedies which the Incas used for healing – she recognised what she had found. It was Sloane too who discovered a way of harvesting its solitary fruit in Cambio's greenhouse. You could say that, without Sloane, there is no Ash Aitkens,' Agent Whittaker mused, as his gaze fell on me. 'Or Fire Boy, for that matter.'

'What happened to her?' said Dmitri. 'Did this Sloane take bite from fruit too?'

'No,' Agent Whittaker explained. 'When Ash Aitkens bombed Cambio Laboratories, Sloane was inside the greenhouse. The explosion ripped through the building and the laboratories surrounding it. When rescuers found her buried beneath the rubble and still alive, they thought it was a miracle. Now we know why.'

Agent Whittaker's expression clouded. When he spoke again, he proceeded slowly, picking his words carefully.

'Paramedics at the scene found a hypodermic needle implanted into Sloane's side. She had removed the last drops of juice-serum from the Tree of the Gods and was injecting it into capsules for safekeeping when the blast hit. How much serum was in the syringe when it entered her bloodstream we cannot say, but Sloane is changed now – utterly transformed – beyond all recognition.'

My insides knotted.

One drop from the Tree of the Gods gave me the power to burn and fly. Two drops turned Ash Aitkens into a man-monkey.

What terrible changes might a larger dose bring about?

That, in a nutshell, was the problem. No one knew. Two days ago, Agent Whittaker informed us, Sloane Sixsmith had walked out of a secure hospital unit in South America. There were guards at the end of each corridor and lobby, bars on the hospital windows and CCTV cameras trained on the exits.

Yet she walked out of the hospital without a single police officer, nurse or doctor seeing her. 'It was as if she disappeared,' Agent Whittaker said with a shake of his head. 'One minute she was there. The next . . . gone.'

'Hold on one second, Mr MI5 man,' Shane Kerrigan spluttered. 'Are you telling us this Sixsmith can make herself invisible?'

Agent Whittaker rubbed his face with the air of a man who could not believe the question he'd been asked or the answer he had to supply. It was an expression I knew well. I saw it every day in maths class whenever I raised my hand.

'The honest answer is we can't rule it out,' Agent Whittaker replied. 'Everyone inside this tent knows what Aidan and his friends can do. We can't take anything for granted.'

My friends!

Sadie and Hussein both shot me a panicked glance. Could Agent Whittaker possibly know about their powers?

'I know what you are thinking,' Mathilde said, stroking Lemon behind the ear. 'Zee answer is yes. Zee Englishman knows about your two friends and their powers.'

'I really wish you'd stop doing that!' I protested.

Mathilde smirked. 'Zee Englishman knows about Lemon too.'

Rule #29 from *The BIG BOOK of Superheroes*:
Heroes who can predict the future are no fun to have around when you're out of luck.

'Terrific,' I muttered.

What Mathilde said was true, much as I hated to admit it. It turned out that since our encounter with Ash Aitkens over a month ago, Agent Whittaker had kept the circus under surveillance. During that time, his agents had spotted Lemon prowling the yard as a tiger and Sadie juggling batons and chasing me around the carousel with the Whack-a-Mole mallet without ever once using her hands.

Hussein's computo-powers almost slipped under the radar. It was his activity online that had tripped him up.

In one month, he turned the gaming world on its head by breaking every gaming record imaginable. In the process, he ran through 25,000 kilowatts of electricity an hour each night, about the same amount of energy Wembley Stadium uses when England plays France under the lights.

Mr Aziz jumped to his feet when he heard this. 'Excuse me, sir. Did I hear you correctly? Did you say twenty-five *thousand* kilowatts an *hour*?'

Agent Whittaker nodded his head sadly. 'You may want to take a very deep breath before you open your electricity bill this month, Mr Aziz.'

Mr Aziz collapsed into his seat. Mrs Aziz buried her head in her hands. Hussein simply groaned.

I had warned him about spending too much time on *Battlegrounds* and *Fortnite*.

The big question now was whether Agent Whittaker would keep our powers a secret or betray us.

For now, at least, he seemed on our side.

'As far as MI5 are concerned, details about Aidan and his friends shall remain strictly confidential,' he claimed. 'I have no intention of informing the Prime Minister or the government about the children's abilities. It is not in their best interests or Britain's. That time will come when they are older. I am also aware that Zarathustra's is considering an offer to move to New York, hence my urgency.'

Agent Whittaker took a deep breath. He glanced round the Big Top slowly seeking out our faces. 'All of us inside this circus tent must pull together. Until we know what powers Sloane Sixsmith possesses, no one is safe. That is why I want you to work for me.'

Everyone spoke at once.

'Hot diggity dog!' Dead-Eye shouted with a slap of her thigh. 'If we all come work for you, does that make us secret agents?'

Finbar Kerrigan smirked. 'You had better check again that there's space for me and my brothers, Mister Agent Man. The last I looked it seemed like there were plenty of clowns already working for the government.'

'You want *children* to work for MI5?' Mum spluttered. 'Are you serious?'

Granny stood and launched into a chorus of 'God Save the Queen' and Atlas slapped his bare chest. 'Atlas is ready!' he roared.

And me?

My ears fizzed. My nose popped. Sparklers shot from my fingertips like it was a wedding day parade!

I was a firecracker ready to go off!

Mathilde turned to me. 'If you burn a hole in zis top, I will place a curse on you zat will turn your hair green and make a river of snot pour out your nose.'

I switched off the sparklers.

'Mathilde, is there any chance—'

'No,' Mathilde said firmly. In her lap Lemon opened one eye briefly, then closed it. 'I will not teach you zis curse, so you can run around school throwing hexes. A curse is like your flames – dangerous and powerful. One must use it with care.'

Green hair and snot curses.

MI5 rocking up with an invitation to the Secret Agent Ball.

A supervillain – on the loose.

It was a lot to take in, and it wasn't even lunch yet.

While I mulled over these revelations, Agent Whittaker took questions from the floor. Granny asked whether MI5 would provide her with a 'licence to kill'. No, was the answer, thank god. Her next question moved on to the possible allocation of firearms. She seemed particularly keen on rocket launchers.

Agent Whittaker stopped her there.

'I am not assembling an elite attack-force comprised of circus stars,' he told her. 'Your mission, should you wish to accept it, has two primary goals. The first is to keep Aidan safe.'

'Keep *me* safe?' I snorted. 'Are you joking?'

Gareth the magician didn't believe it either. 'Have you got this the right way round, man? The lad is the one with the superpower.'

Granny slammed her walking stick down. 'That idiot is the last person we should be protecting,' she growled. 'Do you know how many times he's set fire to the circus tent?'

Three.

'Or the caravans?'

Four.

'Aidan's powers are formidable,' Agent Whittaker agreed. 'But Sloane's may be even stronger.'

There was a smattering of boos and hisses.

'Not possible!' declared Kenise Williams. 'Have you seen the lad fly? Besides, even if it were true, why would she come after Aidan?'

Agent Whittaker remained eerily calm, waiting until everyone was quiet before answering. 'Ask

Aidan yourself. He knows why Sloane will come for him.'

All eyes turned towards me.

'The parcel I received, the one with the jar of Nature's Own,' I sighed. 'Sloane posted it for Ash Aitkens. She addressed it too. Because she never thought I'd open it, she left a message inside for Aitkens and initialled it *SS*. At the time, we didn't know who *SS* was. Now we do.'

This time, there were no jeers. Only silence.

'As I was saying,' Agent Whittaker began again, 'we need to place a safety net around Aidan until we learn more about Sloane's powers and her intentions. Max Goldman and the Americans' offer complicates this. If Zarathustra's travels to New York, MI5 will be unable to protect you. Though we will continue to offer whatever support we can, you will need to look to yourselves for assistance. That is why I am recommending you take Aidan's friends, Sadie and Hussein, with you to New York. Sloane Sixsmith may be able to see through Aidan's Fire Boy disguise, but she will know nothing about Sadie, Hussein or their powers. If we are intent on keeping Aidan safe, that element of surprise may prove essential. Uproar greeted this announcement – mostly from me, Sadie and Hussein who jumped out of our seats and shouted, 'YES!'.

The adults in the room weren't as gung-ho as the three of us, though it was hard to disagree with Agent Whittaker's reasoning. Why send a crack team of undercover operatives when you have a telekinetic with the strength of ten men and a computing wizard on hand? If Sloane Sixsmith was an invisible fighting machine, the more super-powered help I had on hand the better. Especially when it was in the form of two people I trusted.

I didn't wait for the others to make up their minds. I raced towards Sadie and Hussein with my clothes on fire, I was that excited. I was down to a T-shirt and trouser-shorts by the time I reached them.

'Count me in!' Sadie cried.

'You are going to love New York, babes,' Mimi said. She was sure their mum would approve. If nothing else, it would put Sadie and her mother on the same continent.

'Mummy might fly in from Mississippi to see us!' Sadie said excitedly.

'Brilliant!' Hussein replied, glancing timidly at his mother, who seemed unmoved by Agent Whittaker's words. Arms crossed and jaw set, she was having none of it.

'No! I will not allow it,' Mrs Aziz stated fiercely. 'Hussein is too young. He has never been away from home before and this sounds dangerous. How can we let him go to America?'

Agent Whittaker said, 'By keeping Aidan safe, Hussein would be doing Her Majesty's Government a favour.'

'Bah!' Mrs Aziz said with a scowl. 'The government keeps an army doesn't it? Send them to protect Aidan!'

Agent Whittaker ran his hand over the ends of his goatee. 'If Hussein signs on, MI5 can pick up the tab for your electricity bill and write it off as a training exercise.'

'You had best pack warm clothes, Hussein,' Mr Aziz said. 'The winters are cold in New York.' To his wife he added, 'Travel broadens the mind. It is time the boy sees more of the world.'

Sadie and Hussein had their permission slips signed, it seemed. That left one more.

Mine.

When Mum rose to speak, no one – me especially – could predict what she was going to say.

'Correct me if I'm wrong,' she began, 'but it seems you're saying that MI5 cannot protect Aidan *and* keep his identity a secret if he stays in London.'

A few seconds passed before Agent Whittaker replied. 'Unfortunately, that's correct. If MI5 has to provide Aidan with twenty-four-hour protection, my superiors will need to know why.'

'I see,' Mum said. 'Aidan may be safer with the circus, but what about the performers? If Sloane Sixsmith comes after my son, won't they be in danger?'

Before Agent Whittaker could speak, Dmitri stepped forward. 'If Sloane Sixsmith makes war on one of us,' he declared, 'she attacks us all. We are a family and a family stands together.'

One by one, every member of Zarathustra's Travelling Circus, from little Zhang Li to the giant strongman, Atlas, rose from their seats. As they did, each person thrust a fist in the air and said, 'I stand with Aidan.'

Mum was much moved by this show of solidarity.

Her chest heaved. Her eyes teared. She choked back a sob. 'Well,' she said at last. 'New York it is then.'

Me?

I too was much moved too by this call to arms.

When Dmitri said we were a family, a flame burst from my forehead. As each member of the circus stood, the fire spread. My head, arms, shoulders and chest were already blazing by the time Mum spoke.

After that?

Kaboom!

I exploded into flames on the spot.

Evening performances at Zarathustra's usually kicked off just after half-past seven and ended with the Showstopper fireworks after nine.

Friday – Max Goldman night at The Swank – was different. We blitzed through our routines and finished with fifteen minutes to spare. By 9pm sharp we were dressed and out the door.

Taxis (courtesy of Max Goldman) were queuing outside the Big Top to whisk us away. Mum, very smart in a red skirt and black top which Kenise had lent her, waved me over. Our new circus 'members' – Sadie (snazzy in a white party dress) and Hussein (dapper in a buttoned blue shirt and tie) – were already there, waiting. As soon as I arrived (reasonably clean in a Zarathustra's Travelling Circus T-shirt), we piled into a cab.

'Mimi is so jealous we're going to The Swank,'

Sadie said, sliding into the seat next to Mum. 'She insisted I photograph *everything*.'

Hussein took out his phone. 'Mate, take a look at this menu. A *feast* awaits us.'

As I drooled over descriptions of steaks, seafood platters and a dessert tray comprised of chocolate cakes, the passenger door whipped open. 'Move over!' barked Granny, poking me in the ribs with her walking stick. I tried to protest, but her big butt was already inside the cab and headed in my direction. I won't lie. I screamed when her bottom filled my field of vision, Hussein too. We managed to scramble away just in time.

Granny banged her stick against the partition. 'Step on it,' she yelled to the driver. 'I'm hungry!'

The driver glanced anxiously in his rear-view mirror at the She-Bear and off we sped.

Mum gave Granny a telling off, not that it fazed her. Determined to make the most of my night out, I turned my back on her and watched the city streets pass by as we drove along. Christmas lights were strung up over Camden High Street and people spilled on to the footpath outside The World's End pub with pint glasses in their hands. I was so absorbed with the scene outside that I took no notice of Granny until I heard her say to Sadie, 'Pull my finger.'

'NO!' I screamed when I realised what was happening. 'Don't do it!'

I was too late.

As soon as Sadie pulled Granny's finger, the old witch raised her left buttock and let rip with a whopper.

'Ho! Ho! Ho!' Granny cackled, delighted with the stink she made (deadly) and the noise she generated (thunderous).

Quick-thinking Hussein slapped his hand against the door. Immediately every window in the cab – sunroof included – shot open. True, this did startle our driver who had a near-miss with an onrushing bus, but the need for non-toxic breathable air overruled road safety.

I considered flicking Granny with fire in order to teach her a lesson, but decided the risk was too great. Even with the windows down, there was so much gas inside the cab that one flame might send us all to kingdom come. I had forgotten, of course, about Sadie. Using her powers, she bounced Granny up and down on her seat until we reached The Swank. Served her right too.

Our taxi driver pulled up outside its main door where a footman in a waistcoat, trousers and double-breasted coat opened our door. 'This way, please,' he said, leading us up the marble stairs.

The Swank was a six-storey hotel in Mayfair that – to my eye – could have passed for a palace. A grand piano stood beneath a huge chandelier in the lobby. Oil paintings of long-dead lords and ladies lined the walls. Leather armchairs and plush settees were arranged on a polished oak floor. Logs crackled in a fireplace so tall even Atlas could have fit inside it.

The footman led us to the Emperor's Suite where Max Goldman was waiting. Goldman had set up a buffet for us – 'after-show nibbles', he called it – which featured swordfish and lobster, green salads and lentils, sushi and steaks and two cooks in white aprons ready to rustle up whatever else we might want. Champagne flowed (not for me – Mum was watching). A band played songs about New York.

Goldman hopped about the room, shaking hands and greeting people. Dmitri (wearing a white fisherman's jumper – a surprising choice) joined him, explaining who everyone was and what they did. Goldman's assistant, Andrew, fluttered around them both, pouring drinks and taking photos.

To Mathilde (striking in a black military jacket over a leather skirt) Goldman said, 'A fortune-teller, hmm? As soon as we get to New York, you and I need to visit a racetrack.'

To Atlas (brawny as ever in a T-shirt – still in one piece for now) he asked, tapping his biceps, 'Are those real?' Atlas replied by lifting Goldman into the air with one hand.

'Andrew! Photograph!' Goldman cried, preening for the camera.

Granny had headed straight for the bar when she arrived (Mum had pointed her in that direction) so it was just the four of us when Goldman arrived at our table. Dmitri introduced Goldman to Mum, Sadie and Hussein first. Mum's role, Dmitri told him, would be to look after the circus children like me, Sadie and Hussein and help with First Aid.

'Mrs Sweeney, children, it is a pleasure to make your acquaintance,' Goldman said, shaking her hand.

Dmitri placed a hand on my shoulder. 'And this is Mrs Sweeney's son, Aidan. You may know him better as . . . Fire Boy.'

Goldman's eyes lit up. 'THE Fire Boy?'

'It is he,' Dmitri said, beaming like a proud father.

'At last!' Goldman said, rubbing his hands together with glee. 'Come on, kid. Stand up and let me have a look at you.'

I stood.

I stretched my arms out wide.

I swirled round.

I lit my head and hands on fire.

'AHHHHH!' screamed Andrew, dropping the bottle of champagne he was carrying.

Goldman approached me cautiously, hovering his hands over my flames. 'Andrew! Quick! Get me a slice of bread and a fork. I gotta check something.'

Andrew returned seconds later. Goldman skewered the bread and held it over my head with the fork. 'Holy mackerel!' he cried, watching it toast. 'This ain't a trick! Those flames are real. How do you do it, kid?'

'Yes, Aidan. How *do* you make those flames?'

A girl came forward. My age and height, she had

a raspberry jacket thrown on over a black T-shirt. Her eyes were blue and coppery-red hair fell on to her shoulders.

Her teeth were perfect.

Delilah Jones.

Little puffs of smoke popped out of my ears and mouth.

'I–I–I–I . . .'

Dmitri came to the rescue. 'A showman never tells. If we do not keep the secrets of our trade safe, the magic is lost.'

I extinguished my flames.

'And *I* always say, what's the point of having secrets if you can't share them?' Delilah waggled her eyebrow at me, then burst out laughing.

We all laughed too.

Delilah said, 'When Max told me about Fire Boy and Zarathustra's, I hopped on a plane and got here as soon as I could – and boy am I glad I did. It was the BEST night ever!' Breezing past Goldman and Dmitri, she came to a stop directly in front of me. 'Aidan, I swear I could not take my eyes off of you no matter how hard I tried.'

I smiled.

I would have liked to reply with a clever or charming remark – tricky to muster even at the best of times – but I was on new and unfamiliar terrain here and certain that whatever I came up with would only make me sound like the village idiot's dumber cousin.

I smiled some more.

'One of kind, isn't that what I said, Delilah? I knew you'd love him!' piped Max Goldman, throwing an arm around my shoulder – then yanking it away quickly. 'Yow!' Goldman shouted. 'You could fry an egg off this kid.' He looked round quickly. 'Andrew!'

'Yes, Mr Goldman?' asked Andrew, hurriedly appearing over the producer's head.

'Andrew, make a note. Remind me to hose down Hot Stuff here before he meets the old man.' Edging nearer to Delilah, Goldman placed a hand over his heart. 'We don't want to take any chances with Clayton, do we? Your grandfather's well-being must come first.'

'Why, Max Goldman!' Delilah gushed, 'you are just too sweet for words! But there is no need to worry about my granddaddy. He is tougher than horse-hide. And I know this here circus is going to be just the medicine he needs.'

Turning to Dmitri, Delilah said, 'I knew from the moment I walked into the Big Top tonight that this was the right circus for me.'

She extended her hand and Dmitri shook it.

'It looks like you and I are going to be partners,' Delilah grinned.

Our last week in London was manic. Between the final show, stripping the Big Top, packing suitcases and sorting Lemon's crate, it was non-stop.

Agent Whittaker checks in

Our last London performance was on Sunday night. And what a performance it was! What a send-off! We left the centre ring to a standing ovation. Agent Whittaker checked in afterwards, inviting me, Sadie, Hussein and Mum back to Dmitri's caravan for a chat. I was relieved to see he had a new tie on too – pink with blue stripes.

He began by asking how it had gone at The Swank.

'I don't think they'll be asking us back soon,' I replied. Between the conga the Kerrigan brothers led through the lobby, the fight Granny started at the bar, and Eshe and Rodrigo's table-dancing, the Emperor's Suite was in a right state by the time we left. Not that Max Goldman minded. He said it was the best night out he'd had in years. 'You guys are gonna LOVE New York!' he shouted out the window as the police escorted us to our taxis.

'And Delilah Jones?' Agent Whittaker asked. 'How did your meeting go with her?'

'Very well.' I blushed, avoiding Hussein and Sadie's eyes. 'She seemed very keen on the circus.'

Agent Whittaker stretched his long legs. 'Good. Fortunately for us, I am told Delilah is nothing like her grandfather. Avoid dealing with Clayton Jones if you can. He is a ruthless man, a media tycoon who will stop at nothing if he believes it will profit himself or his Frontier News group. If he gets wind of Sloane Sixsmith, or a sniff of anyone else possessing superpowers, he will broadcast it far and wide.'

'Agreed,' Dmitri nodded. 'I will speak only with Goldman and the girl.'

'Is that all you wanted to tell us?' I asked hopefully, crossing my fingers that he wouldn't mention Sloane Sixsmith.

'No,' Agent Whittaker said. 'Sloane Sixsmith was spotted returning to her old flat in Cambio two days ago.'

Oh, fudge.

'The authorities in Peru had guessed she might return. They had the property under surveillance day and night.'

'This is good news though, isn't it?' Mum said. 'At least we know where Sloane is.'

'I'm afraid that, despite the surveillance, Sloane once again disappeared without a trace,' Agent Whittaker admitted. 'I promise I will contact you as soon as I hear anything more.'

Mum and Dmitri thanked him, but the agent waved it away. 'There is something else we need to discuss: the jar of sweets.'

On the outside I remained cool and unflustered.

Inside?

It felt like a volcano had erupted.

As I tried to swallow the smoke that was threatening to escape, I motioned to Agent Whittaker to carry on.

'There is a chance Ash Aitkens was not working alone when he fire-bombed the greenhouse at

Cambio Laboratories. I am still piecing together the details with my South American counterparts, but it appears either a consortium or individual was financing the operation in order to auction off the serum.'

'How much were they hoping to get?' Sadie asked.

Agent Whittaker's eyebrows rose like two drawbridges. 'A billion dollars per sweet.'

A billion dollars! I had swallowed a billion dollars when I drank that serum!

Dmitri whistled.

Mum slapped a hand across her mouth.

Sadie and Hussein gaped at me. *They* had swallowed a billion dollars – each – when they drank that serum!

'Whether Sloane Sixsmith knew about these investors or the auction, I cannot say,' Agent Whittaker admitted. 'Aitkens kept her in the dark whenever possible, but if she did know about the money, there's a good chance she might come looking for that jar of sweets.'

Eyeing me with concern, Agent Whittaker stopped. 'Are you all right, Aidan? Ask away if you like. Is there anything you want to say?'

Say?

Yes, there was something I wanted to say. 'MY *CAT* SWALLOWED A BILLION DOLLARS!'

So long, Caversham

I strolled through Caversham's gates on Monday morning for what I had assumed would be my last week of school for three months, possibly a year. As you might expect, I arrived with a bounce in my step eager to share the news, i.e. that Hussein and I would be swanning off to New York while the rest of my year group – suckers – were stuck here.

Mulch was in the Yard with a circle of flunkies round him. He was in good form himself, it seemed. His parents had finally allowed him to divulge his 'secret' destination – a trip which he had bragged about for weeks that apparently would make us all squirm with jealousy.

As I approached, he made his grand announcement. Mulch was going to New York City.

For two weeks.

And, he crowed, his parents were letting him take two days off school.

Oh, reader. How I laughed. My sides rippled and tiny tears of joy trickled down my cheeks.

'*Two* weeks?' I said to him. '*Two* days off school?'

It was not the reaction Mulch had expected. When I told him about my own plans, his face went white, then green, as envy dripped from every pore in his body. I was only sorry Hussein wasn't here to see it. He was home with the sniffles. Mrs Aziz was taking no chances with her America-bound son and wanted him fit for take-off.

My joy could not restrain itself. When the bell rang, I bounded into class in front of everyone else to tell Miss Spatchcock my good news.

Miss Spatchcock clapped her hands. 'Aidan, I've just heard this morning and I'm nearly as excited as you are! Our little school newspaper is going global. You and Hussein will be our foreign correspondents, our roving reporters in America.'

Like a dog with a bone, Miss Spatchcock was not letting go of this newspaper topic. It was time to rein in expectations, and remind my fellow classmates that they would need to make do without me.

'I promise to cobble a report together *three months from now*,' I said, with an eye-roll of magnificent proportions aimed at the rest of the class as I sat down, 'when I see you next.'

'But Aidan,' Miss Spatchcock said, 'we'll be seeing you in a few days.'

Miss S seemed a bit slow on the uptake this morning. I did my best to bring her down gently.

'I'm afraid not, Miss Spatchcock,' I chuckled, as I took my seat. 'I will be in *New York* for the *next three months*.'

Miss Spatchcock flicked her iPad. 'Have you spoken with your mother?'

I stopped chuckling.

'My mother?'

'Your mother emailed me before school this morning,' Miss Spatchcock informed me with a smile. 'She's going to set up a Zoom link with our class from overseas, so you don't miss out.'

'She WHAT?' I cried.

'Your mother doesn't want you or Hussein to fall behind,' Miss Spatchcock grinned. 'I believe she emailed all your teachers.'

Bloody hell.

Howls of laughter greeted this revolting development. Even Maria Vialli turned round to snigger at me. I rose above it, however. I manfully ignored their taunts. I brushed off the rubbers flicked at me and refused to blink when a wad of paper hit me in the head.

One person wasn't laughing. Stewing in his seat, raising his head only to glare at me, Mulch looked miserable.

Silver linings, eh?

The jar of Nature's Own

Monday afternoon. No show tonight, no rehearsal planned. I celebrated by stretching out on the sofa with a comic book.

Homework, you might say, for an aspiring superhero. Some of the stuff this lot got up to – zipping into other universes, travelling back in time, lifting airplanes – did make me laugh. In my experience, simply flying in a straight line was a challenge if the wind was blowing. I did admire the cut of their costumes though. As I wondered whether Delilah Jones could be persuaded into hooking me up with new gear, Lemon scrambled through her cat flap. A few seconds later, the door swung open and Mathilde walked in.

'Do you always walk in without knocking?' I asked.

'Yes,' Mathilde answered. After snorting when she saw what I was reading, she walked slowly around the main room of our caravan. When she came to my dad's old trunk lying open on the floor, Mathilde stopped. 'Have you started packing yet?'

'No.'

'Good,' she said. 'I have come to talk to you about zee jar of sweets.'

I said nothing.

Mathilde sat down on the floor facing me, her back against the wall. She had no make-up on – no witchy black eyeliner or lipstick – and it made her seem years younger. She was still dressed head to toe in black, of course. Raking the hair out of her eyes, she sighed.

'Agent Whittaker believes your jar of sweets perished when zee monkey-man set off his fire-bomb, *oui*?'

'Yes.'

Lemon padded across Mathilde's outstretched legs and hopped on to the sofa with me.

'How long have you known about the sweets?' I asked.

Mathilde shrugged. 'I am fortune-teller. Zee cards tell me many secrets.'

'I bet they do.' I rolled on to my side. 'What about the others? Do they know there are four sweets left?'

Mathilde shook her head. 'No. Only Dmitri and me. Are you going to take zem to America or . . . ?'

I threw my comic aside and sat up. 'Bury them? Lock them away? I don't know. Is anywhere safe?'

'Take zee jar to America,' Mathilde said, 'but remember, we are travelling by plane. You cannot let people you do not know search your suitcase.'

'Good thinking,' I said.

'Someone must,' Mathilde said. 'If we leave the thinking to you, we are all doomed.'

'Agreed,' I said.

Rule #11 from *The BIG BOOK of Super Heroes*:

Know your limitations. True heroes understand their weaknesses.

'I could hide the sweets in a carry-on bag?' I suggested.

Mathilde shook her head. 'Too risky. You will be searched. I will take zee jar onboard for you if you like.'

I opened my mouth to speak, then stopped.

Mathilde watched me closely. Her lips curled into a thin smile. 'Don't you trust me?' she asked.

'I do,' I said quickly. 'You know I do.'

'But a chance to steal a billion dollars does not come often,' Mathilde said. 'Who would not be tempted?'

'You know about the money?' I cried.

'*Oui*. Knowing is what I do.'

She got to her feet.

'Give your sweets to Sadie to take on zee plane. She will keep zem safe. And when you get to New York, you will need a better stronghold for zis jar than the drawer where you keep your pants.'

I sat up, startled. 'How did you—'

'I know. Beware, little Aidan. Zee next woman who comes for your sweets will not take no for an answer.'

Lemon time

Five suitcases and four carry-on bags waited in the hallway. Next to them was an old army trunk that had once belonged to my father. A blue IKEA bag stuffed with duvets and pillows was slung on top of the trunk and tied shut with twine. Lemon's new cat carrier was there too, peeking out from behind a box marked 'Aidan'.

'This caravan looks like a departure lounge,' Sadie said, surveying the scene.

'I can't believe this is your last night in here,' Hussein said. 'You going to miss it?'

I nodded my head.

I was.

Black on the outside, with orange and red flames painted round its blue windows and door, our caravan wasn't like the others in the park. For the last five weeks, it had been home. Fire Boy's very own Bat Cave. Now it looked like a shell of itself. Its walls were bare, the photos and prints Mum brought from our old flat removed. Its floors had been swept. The kitchen tidied. Our beds stripped.

For now, the forces of Dirt and Grime had been vanquished, but we would soon be departing the field of battle.

By this time tomorrow, Mum and I would be in New York.

Our plane was leaving at dawn. The plan was for Sadie and Hussein to sleep over tonight before waking in the early hours for our trip to the airport. By the time we landed in America, a friend of Dmitri's would have put the circus caravans into cold storage, waiting until we came back.

If we came back.

Dmitri had signed a 'rolling contract' with Max Goldman Enterprises. At the end of three months, Goldman had the option of renewing our contract – extending our three-month stay in New York – or releasing us. He retained that option for one year. That meant Goldman could choose to keep Zarathustra's Travelling Circus (and me) in New York for a year or more.

Imagine.

The next time we see London, Sadie, Hussein and I might be teenagers.

I passed round the sleeping bags. Getting to sleep

tonight wouldn't be easy, but we might as well try.

Lemon ambled over, her tail twitching. She circled the floor in front of us twice before lying down. Lifting her front paw, she glanced at me out of the corner of her eye, a look that said the scratching of her tummy could commence.

Spoilt cat.

I rubbed her soft, furry white belly until she purred.

'Shall we trade places with Lemon?' I asked.

'Yes!' Sadie and Hussein cried.

Crouching next to Lemon on the floor, I scratched her under the ear and whispered, 'Pushkin'.

Lemon's entire body stretched. Her paws grew and grew. Her whiskers lengthened. Her head increased in size. Her ginger hairs spread, growing longer and coarser. Black stripes appeared too. Her tail swished left and right, batting a pillow away. Lemon, a fully grown tiger now, lifted her front paw again.

'It seems her Highness wants the tummy scratching to continue.'

The three of us set to it this time. Lemon rolled on to her tiger back and we rubbed for all we were worth. Soon her eyes closed and she rolled over. Sadie wrapped one of Lemon's front paws over her. Hussein took the back paw. Lying on the floor, propped up against a warm tiger, we turned the TV on. Sadie summoned the sleeping bags over and tucked them in around us.

'This is the life,' Hussein sighed, stroking the hairs on Lemon's paw.

'It's perfect,' Sadie smiled.

For a long time, the TV played and no one said anything. Finally, I asked, 'Are you watching this?'

'No,' Sadie replied.

'Not at all,' Hussein answered.

'Me neither,' I said, flicking the off button on the remote.

And for the rest of the night and long into the morning we talked about New York, Delilah Jones and Sloane Sixsmith.

PART TWO

From the moment our plane touched down in New York, circus life changed. Zarathustra's Travelling Circus had hit the big time.

Crowds of people queued both inside and outside the airport to greet us. Television crews jostled for interviews. Reporters shouted questions and rows of photographers snapped pictures as we walked past. Fans waved signs like **TELL ME MY FORTUNE, MATHILDE** or **FIRE BOY IS HOT!**. Others begged for autographs or asked us to pose for selfies. It took four of us to drag Atlas away from them in the end.

Max Goldman met us at the doors. Andrew was with him, ploughing through the crowds outside so Goldman could stroll untouched behind him. When they reached the scrum surrounding Dmitri, Goldman broke in, waving the microphones away to allow him through. He greeted Dmitri with a hug.

'Zarathustra's has landed!' Goldman barked in his raspy voice. 'The greatest show in the universe is here!' Grinning for the cameras, he placed an arm around Dmitri. 'Brace yourself, New York! You ain't seen nothing like Zarathustra's Travelling Circus and the amazing Fire Boy! Get your tickets while you can!'

A minute later, Goldman, Dmitri and the other performers followed Andrew as he barged a path to the hired coach waiting for us. As we found our seats, Goldman went up and down the aisle, shaking hands and welcoming us to New York.

'How was your flight?' he asked us.

'Eventful,' Mum replied.

Hair-raising, more like. The cabin pressure in the plane had played havoc with Sadie's and Hussein's powers. Lights switched on and off. Bags flew out of the overhead storage. The drinks trolley did a runner from one end of the plane to the other. Between cans of Coke exploding, stewards in a panic and Granny screaming that we were all going to die, it made for a memorable first plane journey.

Deep breathing exercises helped Sadie regain control and a pair of mittens stopped Hussein from shooting off sparks. As for me, it wasn't the pressure inside the airplane that posed a problem. I was used to flying. It was the view. Whenever I looked out the window at the clouds under us, I burst into flames. I couldn't stop myself, no matter how hard I tried. Mum had to shove a sleep mask over my face in the end and wouldn't let me take it off until we landed.

Unlike the airplane ride, the coach ride into New York was top-class. Sadie, Hussein and I sat up front so we could see Manhattan as it came into view.

What a skyline!

Between the skyscrapers and the shops and the people crowding the street corners, I didn't know where to look.

Goldman had the driver take us on a tour round the sights. Faces pressed against the windows, we gaped at the neon lights of Time Square; drove up Broadway where Goldman pointed out all its theatres and down Fifth Avenue where we saw shops wrapped like Christmas presents and hung with fairy lights.

Our tour ended at Central Park.

'Here's your new home!' Goldman cried. 'The most famous piece of real estate in Manhattan – Central Park!'

Inside a huge clearing, away from the zoo, the skate park, the theatre, the playing fields and pond, workers were erecting a maroon-and-gold striped Big Top.

Dmitri stumbled forward. He stared out the coach window at the workers as if he had seen a ghost. 'Max, how can this be? When we left London this morning, our tent was on a trailer. How can it be here . . . and so big?'

'Surprise!' Andrew cried, hopping out of his seat and clapping his hands. Pulling out his phone, he took Dmitri's picture.

Goldman skipped about on his little legs. 'Look at his face!' he grinned. 'I told you he wouldn't believe it! Come on! Follow me! You've got to see this!'

Goldman stormed down the steps of the coach. Dmitri staggered after him. Whether it was the shock of seeing the new Big Top or the jet lag I can't say, but the old Russian looked unsteady on his feet. As soon as he stepped outside, the rest of us piled out, following the pair of them (and Andrew) down the grooved runway that had been placed over the grass and led to the tent.

Standing in front of the entrance, Goldman posed with his arms over his chest as Andrew scampered about snapping photos. 'When Max Goldman says he can make wishes true, he does not joke around. Dmitri, say hello to your new Big Top!'

'Unbelievable!' cried Grandpa Yang.

'Wow,' gasped Shane Kerrigan.

'Zis I expected,' shrugged Mathilde. 'A vision of zis tent came to me in a dream.'

Mathilde aside, it was a right shock to the rest of us. Towering over us, right here in New York City was Zarathustra's Big Top – the same markings, the same entrances and exits, the same centre posts – only twice as big and brand-spanking new.

'It's custom-made,' Goldman said, running his hand over the tent's flap. 'The canvas is sailcloth and made of carbon fibre – you could sail around the world in this tent. Plus, it's coated in industrial fireproof material in case our fiery friend here happens to take a wrong turn.'

'He's seen you fly,' Hussein sniggered.

I opened my mouth to blow smoke into his face only to find Mum giving me The Stare.

A short note on The Stare:

The Stare is a wide, two-eyed glare imbued with a frightening intensity. A pre-emptive strike often employed in social settings, The Stare operates as a cease-and-desist order informing me to think again, i.e. that should I persist in my anticipated actions, there will be consequences.

I swallowed the smoke.

I followed Dmitri inside the circus tent. Like him, my jaw dropped and my eyes opened wide. This was an indoor *arena*, not a Big Top. You could fit thousands of fans in here!

'Come on! This way!' Goldman cried. 'There's more! There's more!'

We followed him and Andrew out the side exit and came face-to-face with a caravan park.

Arranged in the same order as they'd been in London, and decorated in the same colours and styles, were our caravans.

Only it wasn't really them. These caravans were new and bigger.

Much bigger, in fact.

Dmitri's maroon and gold caravan came with a gilded extension. Mathilde's black caravan, decorated with tarot cards, neon lights and witchy symbols, was now the Fortune House, a tiny gothic mansion. Our own black caravan with its orange and red flames and blue door now came with a second storey.

'Look, Mum,' I yelled, tugging her arm. 'They super-sized our caravan!'

Goldman bounced over, a smug grin slapped across his face and a cigar in his hand. 'If you want to be big, you gotta think big. Get used to it, kid. It's the American way.'

Dmitri placed a hand over his heart. His twinkly eyes misted. 'Max Goldman, on behalf of Zarathustra's Travelling Circus, I struggle to find right words to thank you for all you have done.'

Puffing on his cigar, Goldman's grin widened. 'Dmitri, believe me, I would love to take credit for this circus village, but it was all Delilah's doing. She gave satellite photos of your London site to the builders and told them to have it completed before you arrived. Said she wanted New York to feel like home – only better.'

Better sounded good – pretty darn good, from where we were standing.

'There's more space to chase my brothers,' Shane Kerrigan said of the giant playhouse of a caravan Delilah had made the Krazy Klowns.

Atlas tore his T-shirt in two and slapped his chest. 'Caravan gym is like Atlas – tall and strong!'

'I can see the West Side from my balcony,' Kenise Williams cooed.

While we marvelled at our new surroundings and Max Goldman puffed on his cigar, a skateboarder in a hoodie and shorts whizzed towards us. Leaping over steps and boarding down railings, the skater came to a sudden stop in front of us, flipping the skateboard into her hands.

The skater unbuckled her helmet, shaking red hair loose, swishing it from side-to-side.

Reader, it was like being on the film set of a shampoo ad. All we needed was slo-mo and music playing in the background. I didn't know whether to say hello or applaud.

'Delilah!' Goldman exclaimed. He licked his fingers and slicked back his few remaining strands of hair. 'We were just talking about you.'

Delilah slid her skateboard into her backpack while everyone spoke at once. We thanked her for the new Big Top, the caravans, the larger-than-life carousel and the carnival games – all near-replicas of the London versions, only bigger and better.

Delilah smiled, searching through the beaming faces crowded round her until she found the one she was looking for.

Mine.

'Welcome to New York,' she said.

A few minutes later, I was airborne.

I flew over the rows of brand-new, empty bleachers. Fiery arms outstretched, I circled one of the centre posts, a tail of shimmering sparks trailing after me. I soared higher, zigging in and out of the Big Top's tall rafters. Three somersaults, a corkscrew spin and a jack-knife turn later, I began my slow descent.

'How's that?' I asked Delilah, hovering above her.

'Aidan Sweeney,' she said breathlessly, staring up at me, her eyes like two white saucers with a cornflower-blue middle. 'I am lost for words.'

I glowed firecracker-red.

I blazed so bright that the small group who had followed Delilah and me into the Big Top had to shield their eyes.

'Thank you,' Delilah gushed. 'I apologise for dragging you in here, but I just *had* to see you fly and there was no way I could wait a week until the circus opens. Ever since this little ol' Big Top went up, I've been waiting to see you inside it. I hope you don't mind.'

'Ho, ho,' I chuckled in mid-air, my fiery hands on my fiery hips. 'It's no trouble. After all, flying is what I do best.'

A list of responses to this exchange with Delilah Jones:

- A loud snort accompanied by a narrowing of eyes (Sadie)
- A gagging gesture, i.e. a finger pointed towards his open mouth (Hussein)

- An arched eyebrow and tiny smirk which meant she either found me amusing or I was digging a hole so deep for myself I might never get out (Mum)
- An eye-roll of *magnifique* proportions (Mathilde)
- A rude hand gesture one normally associates with away fans at a football match (Granny)
- A neck-scratching frown directed at the Big Top above me (Dmitri)

Delilah was still beaming a smile (perfect in every way) at me.

'Aidan Sweeney, I could watch you fly day and night and still come back for more,' she gushed.

My flames flared.

'Do you want *my* honest opinion?' Sadie piped up.

'No,' was my equally truthful answer. I was, at that moment, very happy basking in the sunlight of Delilah's smile and quite content to remain there.

'Your flames seem smaller,' Sadie said, ignoring me and carrying on regardless. 'Whether it's you or the air in here I don't know.'

'Smaller?' I squawked.

'Better lay off the crisps too, mate,' Hussein added. 'You're looking slow going around the bends.'

Slow?

I gathered a ball of flames in my hand and prepared to take aim.

'Hussein and Sadie are right,' Dmitri grunted.

'They are?' I cried, extinguishing my flames and landing swiftly.

'The Big Top you build for us is wonderous, Miss Jones,' Dmitri confided. 'I am very moved. But bigger tent is challenge. Like great new circus tent, Zarathustra's itself must become bigger.'

'How will we do that?' I asked.

Dmitri eyes twinkled. 'Do not worry. We will find way.'

Late night.

A text message sent from Delilah Jones to Aidan Sweeney at 9:41pm:

You awake? It's me. D

A text message sent from Aidan Sweeney to Delilah Jones at 9:42pm:

Yeah. How'd you get my number?

A text message sent from Delilah Jones to Aidan Sweeney at 9:43pm:

I rang the network. It helps when your granddaddy owns it. LOL.

A text message sent from Aidan Sweeney to Delilah Jones at 9:44pm:

Nice.

A text message sent from Delilah Jones to Aidan Sweeney at 9:44pm:

Aidan. Can I ask you a question?

A text message sent from Aidan Sweeney to Delilah Jones at 9:45pm:

Fire away.

A text message sent from Delilah Jones to Aidan Sweeney at 9:46pm:

How'd you get your power?

A text message sent from Delilah Jones to Aidan Sweeney at 9:46pm:

I won't tell anyone I promise. EVER. I will take it to the grave. Swear to God and hope to die. 🙌

A text message sent from Aidan Sweeney to Delilah Jones at 9:47pm:

I'm sorry, Delilah. I promised my mum that I would never tell. Dmitri too. I gave them my word and can't go back on it. 😫

A text message sent from Aidan Sweeney to Delilah Jones at 9:50pm:

Delilah, you still there?

A text message sent from Aidan Sweeney to Delilah Jones at 9:52pm:

Delilah?

Early morning

Dmitri received an email from Agent Whittaker at four in the morning.

It concerned Sloane Sixsmith.

Somehow Sloane had evaded the South American authorities in Cambio. They did, however, find a notebook which she'd left behind containing a timetable and travel plans.

After Cambio, Sloane intended to fly to Los Angeles.

On the same day that Zarathustra's opened its Big Top in Central Park to crowds, Sloane hoped to be in London.

Her last stop?

New York City.

rehearsals

Opening night was one week away.

We had seven days to adapt our routines into new acts that filled Zarathustra's brand-new Big Top arena.

'In New York we must move from small church to great cathedral,' Dmitri said when we assembled the next morning. 'Sound. Lights. Movement. Everything must change. We must make ourselves like giants so children in distant seats can see.'

Dmitri meant every word. We restaged our opening number (the Grand Parade); we reset the dance steps and timings for our exit (the Showstopper); and rewrote everything in-between.

For acts rooted to the ground like Gareth the magician and Atlas, Dmitri had to allow more time for entrances and exits. Positions on the floor were altered. Props were arranged differently around the ring.

For airborne acts like myself, the changes were more significant. The dance trapeze act, Eshe and Rodrigo, had to amend their routine because the taller centre posts altered the trajectory of their rope-swing. Kenise Williams had to rethink her steps due to the longer tight rope. And the Red Arrows had to re-choreograph their trampoline routine to make greater use of the space around them.

My problem was speed. Either I was too slow – hovering over the larger open space like a fiery zeppelin, or too fast – whipping round bends like I had been shot out of a cannon. I also discovered that whenever I flew faster, I burnt brighter. Rehearsing morning, noon and night was hard work, but as the days passed our acts became tighter. I could feel my powers growing too. By the end of the week, I had almost forgotten what it felt like to fly inside the smaller Big Top back in London. Now that I felt confident in the fast lane, I had no intentions of ever slowing down again.

Dmitri noticed.

'Slow down! Slow down!' he cried as I buzzed

past overhead. 'There's no need to go so fast.'

I couldn't help myself. Inside the new Big Top, I was a flaming bullet, a human comet with a tail of flames fanning out behind me. I had no intention of ever slowing down again. True, more speed brought more risk. Nosedives gave me nosebleeds when I hit full throttle. Super-fast somersaults and loop-the-loops at top speed left me dizzy, but I battled on. If I was going to be America's next great circus star, I had to pay the price and rehearse, rehearse, rehearse.

Luckily for me, I had Hussein about to keep me company. Knowing we'd need the best sound and lighting in the business to make our circus rock, Dmitri decided to go with superpowers over experience. He handed Hussein the keys to the control booth – and what a sound and light show he and his computo-powers delivered! Strobe lights, fog machines, bubble makers, laser lights, twirling spotlights and a concert sound-system that boomed music and sound effects came to life, all with a touch of his fingers.

The special effects Hussein cooked up for Mathilde's entrance alone – bats bursting out of the windows of a haunted house and swooping over the audience as thunder rumbled and lightning crackled – was worth the price of admission. It left Dmitri gaping at the illuminations overhead.

'What strange magic is this?' he gasped, shuddering as a final lightning bolt lit up the Big Top.

'This is nothing,' Hussein said casually. 'Wait until you see what I have planned for The Showstopper.'

While Hussein was busy revolutionising Zarathustra's special effects, Sadie had taken on a more covert role.

On the day we arrived in New York, we discovered private security guards installed on the circus premises – big, beefy men in black uniforms with orders to keep trespassers away. Each of them wore body armour, had a radio earpiece plugged in and carried holstered firearms, pepper spray, handcuffs *and* tasers. Granted, you wouldn't get anyone wandering in asking for autographs or selfies with these lads about, but that didn't matter to Dmitri. 'Soldiers do not belong in circus,' was his line and nothing Max Goldman said about paparazzi, Central Park or media interest in Zarathustra's could convince him otherwise.

Not that his protests mattered.

Hidden in the fine print of our contract was a clause granting Frontier News and Media the rights to employ as much private security as they deemed necessary to protect their 'assets' – us. We were stuck with them.

That's where Sadie came in.

'Your powers, they make things move, yes?' Dmitri said with a sly smile. 'Soldiers do not like things that go bump in the night. Maybe we can make Zarathustra's a place these security guards do not want to be.'

A wicked gleam came into Sadie's dark eyes.

'Speak to Mathilde,' Dmitri grinned. 'She may have a suggestion or two on how you can frighten these men.'

Seeing Sadie and Mathilde locked in conversation or hooting with laughter like two witches on a night out, I almost felt sorry for the security squads.

Almost.

Whatever the two of them had planned, Sadie wasn't telling. 'Wait and see,' is all she said.

The rest of rehearsal week was spent bunking down in our new caravan. Granny had bagged the bedroom on the ground floor for herself, Mum and Sadie nabbed the double bedroom upstairs and Hussein and I got the bunk bed in the middle room. Lemon moved from room to room, sniffing its new furniture warily. Change, it seemed, did not agree with her.

Rehearsals went on well into the night, so Hussein and I didn't have much time for sightseeing our first week. We made do with Central Park and the streets that bordered it.

Unlike us, Sadie wasn't tied down to the Big Top. She and Mum hit the sights: a show on Broadway, a climb to the top of the Empire State Building, a wander round The Metropolitan Museum of Modern Art and waffles and ice cream at Carte Blanche.

I put my foot down.

Missing the odd landmark I could live with. Museums? Help yourselves.

But waffles and ice cream? *That* was taking it too far.

Rule #6 from *The BIG BOOK of Superheroes*:
Even superheroes have to eat.

I insisted – nay, *demanded* – that Mum take Hussein and I out for lunch too. And so, on day four, Mum took us to my choice of eateries, Alejandro's: Home of the Giant Taco, for lunch. While Hussein and I crunched through nachos, Mum told us about her outings with Sadie.

Mum's highlights (in no particular order) of the previous days of escorting Sadie around New York:

- The compliments bestowed on them from strangers who assumed they were mother and daughter, e.g. tributes to their youth and beauty, the warmth of their relationship, the sparkle of their conversations, etc.
- Sadie's enthusiasm for the works of Pollock, Basquiat, Warhol and others as they glided through The Metropolitan Museum of Modern Art
- The exquisite table manners of her dining companion

– The hours they spent in Sak's Fifth Avenue after lunch, browsing the shoes, commenting on clothes and trying the free ointments and make-up on offer

I placed my Giant Taco down (even with two hands it was hard to hold without the sauce spilling out of its ends) and looked at Hussein. 'Three days walking around museums and shoe shops?'

'BOR-ING!' we chanted together.

Mum watched Sadie pick at her salad and sighed wistfully.

I said, 'Sadie might know about art, but I bet she can't do this.' Grabbing two straws off the table, I stuck them up my nose as I let rip with my howler monkey imitation – the one where I scratched my sides and whooped.

It had Hussein in stitches. He was laughing so hard he nearly coughed up his burrito.

Mum was less amused.

I didn't mind.

I was in a good mood.

Tomorrow night was Press Night. For the first

time ever, our new Big Top would open its doors to New Yorkers of all ages.

Get ready, America. Zarathustra's Travelling Circus was here!

Did I mention that Delilah had texted me back?

Delilah had texted back the next night.

A text message sent from Delilah Jones to Aidan Sweeney at 10:31pm:

Hi. You up?

A text message sent from Aidan Sweeney to Delilah Jones at 10:31pm:

Yes.

A text message sent from Delilah Jones to Aidan Sweeney at 10:32pm:

Want to play a game?

A text message sent from Aidan Sweeney to Delilah Jones at 10:32pm:
Sure.

A text message sent from Delilah Jones to Aidan Sweeney at 10:33pm:
It's called Guess. I try to guess how you got your superpower and you tell me if I'm right or wrong.

A text message sent from Aidan Sweeney to Delilah Jones, at 10:33pm:
You'll never win.

A text message sent from Delilah Jones to Aidan Sweeney at 10:34pm:
We shall see about that, Mr Fire Boy! I do love a challenge!

A text message sent from Aidan Sweeney to Delilah Jones at 10:36pm:
Does this game come with rules?

A text message sent from Delilah Jones to Aidan Sweeney at 10:37pm:

There are two rules to Guess. One, I am allowed only one guess each day. Two, if I'm right you must tell the truth.

A text message sent from Aidan Sweeney to Delilah Jones at 10:38pm:

You're on. Let's play.

A text message sent from Delilah Jones to Aidan Sweeney at 10:38pm:

You mean it? You're not messing with me?

A text message sent from Aidan Sweeney to Delilah Jones at 10:39pm:

I like games. Go on. Guess.

A text message sent from Delilah Jones to Aidan Sweeney at 10:40pm:

Aidan Sweeney, tell me the truth: were you born on another planet?

A text message sent from Aidan Sweeney to Delilah Jones at 10:41pm:

Friday was Press Night, the first night we were throwing open our doors to a live audience – and, Max Goldman warned us, it was going to be a bare-knuckle ride.

Goldman waltzed into the Big Top near noon to check on last-minute preparations. He brought bagels and cream cheese for everyone – 'They settle the nerves' – which his assistant, Andrew, dished out.

'What is "Press Night"?' I asked, tearing into my bagel.

'It's the night New York's theatre critics show up,' Goldman explained. 'In this town, reviews can make or break a show, so it's very important. If your show gets panned on Press Night, it might close before it opens.'

Sadie said, 'Who are these critics?'

'Who are they?' Goldman's smile vanished. His eyes went cold. His face turned red. 'Who are they?' he repeated, snarling, clenching his fists. 'Bloodsucking leeches, that's who they are. Harpies with pens. Cold-hearted, joyless gargoyles who sit in the seats I paid for and tell ME—'

'Mr Goldman, sir!' cried Andrew, fluttering behind him. 'Remember what Dr Feinstein said about your blood pressure. You need to walk away, sir, and take a time out.'

As Goldman's colouring moved from an alarming purply-red back to normal, Andrew whispered over his head, 'It's best not to talk about critics in front of Mr Goldman.'

We nodded and finished the bagels in silence.

The rest of the afternoon was spent watching the clock in nervous anticipation. Gradually, the sun set and the spotlight aimed at the outside of the Big Top flicked on.

Showtime neared.

Though I tried not to peek out the caravan windows, it was impossible not to. A crowd I expected, but not a queue forming hours – yes, hours – before we went on.

The line to get in stretched as far as the eye could see!

Reporters took up spots outside the gate, pointing microphones at people who passed.

Stretch limos ferried celebrities into the grounds. Chauffeurs raced to open their doors as stars of stage and screen swaggered out, blowing kisses to star-struck fans.

One Rolls Royce drove into the Big Top itself, stopping at the VIP box seats at ringside.

'Holy mackerel!' cried Goldman, peeping out from behind the curtains. 'It's Mr Big Pockets himself! Clayton Jones is here with Delilah! No one has seen him for over a month. I didn't think his doctors let him leave his sickbed these days.' Goldman licked his fingers and patted down the six strands of hair combed over the top of his head. 'How do I look?'

'Stunning, sir,' gushed Andrew.

'Very smart,' I said. Goldman did look the part in his white tux and bow-tie.

'Wish me luck,' he said. 'I'm going over there to welcome Clayton Jones to the Big Top.'

Delilah hopped out of the Rolls before the driver

could open her door, then raced over to the other side to help her grandfather out. Clayton Jones was a white-haired man with wild, uncombed hair. He stepped forwards uncertainly, his black eyes darting angrily from side to side as he shuffled to his ringside seat. Delilah sat down next to him, chatting away as Goldman walked over with his arms open wide in greeting. When Delilah caught me poking my head through the curtains, she waved.

I ran back to the dressing room.

It was buzzing with pre-performance excitement. Most of the cast were already in their costumes or applying their last licks of make-up.

On a chair next to my Fire Boy costume, I found a large, gift-wrapped box. Wrapped in gold paper, it had flame-coloured ribbons and a big bow. Its card said: Aidan

I ripped it open.

Inside the box was a new costume – a Protecto-Wear II (Combat Grade) in firecracker-red with black swirls. The tail was forked, its horns were pointed.

I slipped it on.

The new Protecto-lining added bulk to my

physique, making me appear as if I had muscles. When I looked in the mirror, the image staring back at me seemed positively *evil*.

There was only one person in the world who loved comic books as much as me – and had the money to pay for a costume like this.

Delilah.

'Hel-lo,' said Shane Kerrigan, half his face painted clown-white. 'Who is this masked demon I see before me?'

'I think Atlas has been slipping him protein shakes on the sly,' Donal added with a wink.

Finbar smiled at me as he laced his giant shoe. 'Do you like it?'

'Like it? I LOVE IT!' I whooped. Swivelling round to face the mirror, I gave it my best Atlas-pose. 'I might never take it off.'

Shane, Donal and Finbar hopped up and joined me in front of the mirror. Soon everyone followed suit – Mathilde, Kenise, Eshe and Rodrigo, Gareth, the Red Arrows (synchronised flexing – how do they do it?) and Dead-Eye – showing off our muscles for all we were worth. How Atlas laughed!

Dmitri didn't, I'm afraid. 'What are you doing?'

he shouted as he rushed in the door while we were posing. 'We're on in five minutes!' he shouted, pulling his hair.

Sure, we were a little late, but I think a laugh or two backstage always helps. We needed it too. No one knew what to expect.

Could we pull this off?

In the end, we aced it.

Kenise Williams wowed crowds with her tightrope act. The Krazy Klowns were on top form. Gareth the magician left his audience spellbound and the future held no fear for Mathilde. Hussein's sound and light show had the audience tapping their toes or gaping open-mouthed at his effects.

Sitting in the dressing room, I didn't need the volume turned up on the monitor to hear the crowd's response. Applause rattled the walls. The first time I flew in through the doors, the explosion of cheers almost snuffed out my flames!

What a show!

What a circus!

Max Goldman danced into the dressing room afterwards. 'You did it! You did it! They loved us!' he cried, jumping into Dmitri's arms and kissing him on the forehead. 'The show will run for years and years!'

As Goldman went from person to person in the dressing room, locking each of them in an embrace, Andrew slipped me a card. 'Ms Jones told me to deliver this into your hands personally,' he said.

It said:

I borrowed a pen off Andrew. Flipping the card over, I wrote:

I looked nervously at the letter 'A' floating underneath the line. It seemed lonely, so I scrawled a tiny x after it and hurriedly handed the card to Andrew. I asked if he wouldn't mind taking it back to Delilah.

Andrew clutched it to his chest, sighing theatrically. 'But, soft, what light through yonder window breaks? It is the east, and Delilah is the sun.'

I scowled at him Fire Boy-style – two snorts of steam billowed out of both nostrils while flames shot out of my hair and eyebrows.

Andrew took the hint and exited stage left.

Max Goldman was right about the newspapers mentioning Clayton Jones. The next day, photographs of him entering the circus made every front page in New York.

BILLIONARE VISITS BIG TOP

Clayton Jones III, the ailing billionaire chairman of Frontier News and Media, left his luxury apartment on Fifth Avenue for the first time in many weeks yesterday to visit the CIRCUS! Jones, who is 64 years old, was escorted into the Big Top by his granddaughter, Delilah. Jones joined a packed audience to see the flaming sensation, FIRE BOY, make his first New York appearance as Zarathustra's Travelling Circus opened its three-month run in Central Park.

Under the article there was a picture of Jones being helped into the back seat of his Rolls Royce by a beaming Delilah.

Zarathustra's Travelling Circus got a write-up in all the major New York papers too. Those critics Max was so worried about? They *loved* us!

Zarathustra's Travelling Circus is a virtuoso of energy and pizzazz, topped off by a red-hot performance by Fire Boy. If this fiery daredevil doesn't get you out of your seat, nothing will.

Myron Humbug, The New York Times

Who would have thought New York's most amazing stage show would be found under the Big Top in Central Park? When you see Zarathustra's amazing Fire Boy, you will truly BELIEVE a boy can fly!

Wendy Bakstabbir, *Daily Herald*

Amazing! I have never seen anything like Fire Boy of Zarathustra's Travelling Circus and I cannot wait to go again.

I. M. Board, The Daily News

A couple more reviews like that and Max Goldman might have a few kind words to say about theatre critics!

Our celebrations, however, ended there.

Ever since Agent Whittaker pulled me out of school, I had been waiting for Sloane Sixsmith to appear.

That morning she did.

When Mum told us Dmitri asked me back to his caravan, I assumed he wanted to congratulate me on last night's performance. Instead we found every member of the circus inside and waiting for us.

We found a seat at the back and sat down quickly.

Dmitri began by telling us how proud he had been of Zarathustra's last night. We had thrilled a hard-to-please audience and soon news of our great circus would spread from New York to San Francisco.

But that wasn't why he had called us together. Agent Whittaker had emailed Dmitri again. This time the email contained a video which MI5 had obtained. He wanted Dmitri to share it with us.

I waited for Shane Kerrigan (or one of his brothers) to make a joke and ask if Agent Whittaker had sent us MI5's Guide to New York City or the latest episode of *Strictly Come Dancing*.

But he didn't.

No one spoke.

Dmitri flicked on the big screen in the centre of the room.

I could feel Mum tense beside me. Even Granny grunted nervously while Sadie reached a hand out to me and Hussein. We took them as the room hushed and the video started.

I was surprised at how ordinary Sloane seemed.

At first.

Sloane had a small face with a turned-up nose and sallow cheeks. Her hair was cut straight, falling to her shoulder in mousey-brown sheets. She had a square mouth and hazel brown eyes. She wore a faded T-shirt with planet Earth embossed on it in blue and green. What stood out most was the room around her. It was more jungle than room. Vines hung from the ceiling and her desk was covered in ferns. The room itself seemed hot too, sweltering. Strands of hair clung to her forehead. Her T-shirt was damp with sweat.

And then she spoke.

Hola. My name is Sloane Sixsmith, environmental scientist and survivor of the explosion at Cambio Laboratories – yes, that *Cambio Laboratories.*

You will be glad to hear that I am now in a position to confirm that my initial hypothesis on el Árbol de los Dioses *was correct. Its unique biochemical components do indeed act as a trigger, modifying a person's genetic code in the most extraordinary way. I know this because three vials of this concentrated serum are currently circulating through my veins.*

On-screen, Sloane's hair shortened into spikes. Snake-like scales emerged on her skin. Her eyes turned yellow and her scales darkened into a brownish-green.

Inside the caravan, there were gasps and cries and, from Granny, a few choice swear words.

The fiery heat deep down in my belly, the spark which the serum from *el Árbol de los Dioses* had lit months ago, went ice-cold.

I gripped Sadie's hand more tightly as Sloane Sixsmith ran her claws over her bright scales.

The results are most amazing, wouldn't you say?

There are drawbacks. The room temperature is a balmy thirty degrees in here, and I would prefer it hotter still. I need sunlight regularly and, as you may have guessed from my furnishings, I am drawn towards tropical habitats. My dietary habits appear to be changing too.

Sloane snapped a twig off a plant and began nibbling at it.

My teeth ached watching her.

There are advantages though.

Sloane's features changed again. Her scales disappeared. Her nose became round, her hair black and curly. Her face morphed into a pink-skinned, thick-necked man. When Sloane spoke, her voice was a low rumble.

This man's name is Roger Fudd. I ran into him yesterday in Los Angeles. He held the door for me as I got into a cab. So polite. I laid a hand on his shoulder and thanked him. When I returned to my hotel and looked into a mirror, this is the reflection that greeted me.

I knew his name. I remembered the holidays he spent as a child in Iowa. I understood why he hadn't spoken to his older brother, Henry, since he left home. Roger's memories were my *memories.*

I am no longer one person. I am many.

Sloane changed into a young blonde-haired woman with scarlet lips; a perspiring, heavy-set, red-faced man; an old grey-haired, brown-skinned woman. Whenever she shape-shifted, Sloane introduced the person by name and told us who they were, what they wanted to do with their lives, their happiest moments and their sorrows.

In their own voices too.

It was like a one-woman stage show where Sloane was each character – and I mean literally *was* each person – right down to their skin, hair, nose, mouth and body.

Soon I will know your dark, dirty secrets too. Who you cheated. Who you deceived. Who you stepped over to get your way.

Sloane's features reshaped themselves to form the same sallow face that opened the video.

All it takes is a touch.

I'll be arriving in London shortly. See if you can stop me.

The video ended.

How long we sat in stunned silence inside Dmitri's caravan, I can't say. It seemed like ages.

Finally, Granny spoke.

'*This* is your supervillain?' she hooted, throwing her head back and laughing. 'A lizard woman with a long tongue?'

Dead-Eye began to chuckle. Finbar Kerrigan joined in and soon we were all laughing, even wise old Grandpa Yang, arms crossed and chin upon his chest.

Mathilde sneered. 'Come clubbing with me on Saturday night. I will show you far worse than zis Sloane.'

Donal Kerrigan stood. 'One touch,' he said in a throaty voice that could have passed for Sloane's. 'It's all I need.' Laying his hand on Atlas's head, he puffed out his chest and began strutting about, flexing his scrawny arms and lifting a water bottle over his head like it weighed a tonne.

'Sign her up, Dmitri!' Gareth the magician urged from the back. 'Crowds love impressionists!'

Kenise Williams winked at Eshe. 'She can do Stormzy for me anytime.'

While the two of them snickered, Shane Kerrigan bounded after his brother, hopping from bench to bench like a lizard, his eyes big and sticking his tongue out as if hunting for flies.

Dmitri put two fingers into his mouth and whistled. 'Enough! Back to your seats!'

It was like being back in a classroom (except that

circus people listened and did what they were told).

Dmitri fixed us with a dead-serious stare that no one dared break. 'Sloane is not a Kraken, a monster raised from the sea. She is not a beast who brings plague to our cities or a great warrior who no army can defeat. She is far worse.'

I glanced at Sadie and Hussein. What could be worse than monsters, plague or war?

Dmitri studied the frozen image of Sloane staring out at us from her jungle room on the screen behind him.

'If this woman shakes my hand, she can walk away with *me*, Dmitri – everything that makes me who I am, not just my appearance but my memories . . . of you all, of my precious Zarathustra, of the places I've been, and more than that too. My desires, fears, dreams, regrets.'

Dmitri's eyebrows bunched together. His mouth straightened into a grim line.

He looked afraid.

'I do not want a stranger to gaze into my soul,' he declared. 'We open our hearts to the people we love, not anyone we bump into on the street. We should be able to choose who we share our lives, our memories with. No one,' he said firmly, 'has the right to take that choice away from us.'

Nobody dared joke after that.

'Maybe Agent Whittaker stops Sloane in London, yes? This we hope. But we must prepare for worst.'

A sombre mood settled over us as we debated how best to combat the threat Sloane Sixsmith posed. Eventually, we decided on a three-part plan:

How to spot and stop a shape-shifter:

LOCK: Caravans and wardrobes need to be locked at all times. As Sadie notes, Sloane Sixsmith might be able to change from a size 6 to a size 16 in seconds, but the clothes she had on remained the same. If Sloane wants to impersonate us, she has to pilfer our clothes. Keep the clothes (and costumes) under LOCK and key, and we will never be fooled.

STOCK: Vigilance is necessary. Odd behaviours or unusual requests should not be ignored. We must take STOCK at all times.

SHOCK: Circus performers must travel in pairs whenever leaving the circus grounds. This will prevent Sloane from nipping back into the circus grounds in disguise. True, being forced to travel in pairs will be a SHOCK to the system – whoever gets Granny on a night out is drawing the very shortest of straws – but needs must.

Lock, Stock and Shock. I strode out of Dmitri's caravan with my head high. There's nothing like an action plan to keep shape-shifters away.

broadway

Life comes at you pretty fast when you're a circus star on Broadway – or off-Broadway (which is the category Central Park fell under). You couldn't go far without seeing a poster, billboard or shop window with FIRE BOY on it.

Poster boy

Fire Boy had become the official face for Zarathustra's Travelling Circus. Ads of me flying over Central Park started appearing on TV, in newspapers and online with a **Be Afraid. Be Very Afraid. Fire Boy is Here** tagline.

On the same day the carousel arrived – Max Goldman insisted on limiting the grounds outside the Big Top to a carousel, food stands and souvenir booths – a delivery van dropped off a shedload of Fire Boy merchandise.

A list of Fire Boy merchandise on sale at Central Park:

- Flame-coloured Fire Boy T-shirts, sweatshirts, hats, scarves and pyjamas
- Fire Boy demon masks ('Perfect for frightening the neighbours')
- A Fire Boy barbecue kit that came with a flaming apron and quick-fire charcoals
- Two different types of Fire Boy action figures: 'Flyer' (who wore a cape) and 'Smokey' (squeeze his tummy and smoke pops out of his bum)
- RED-HOT Fire Boy Tabasco sauce. This was top-notch. Put a few drops of that on your cheese sandwich and . . . *Voila!* You have transformed a slice of cheese and two pieces of buttered bread into a culinary delight

And then there was @fireboy.

The Fire Boy Instagram account was Goldman's idea, a way of generating publicity for Zarathustra's. Sadie wanted a crack at running it, so I gave her free rein. It was *her* decision not to take it seriously. Sadie's Fire Boy confessed that he was afraid of spiders (true); shared pictures of how toast should look – burnt and black; added comments like 'Yum' or 'That looks good' to videos of barbecues or roast dinners that ended in flames; and ridiculed water sports.

The last I checked, my @fireboy account had over 100k followers.

Home-Schooling

Now that the all-day rehearsals were over, Mum had decided it was time to open Miss Spatchcock's 'Box of Treats'. First up was a writing task asking us to describe 'A New York moment which you will always remember'. Mum handed out paper and told us we had an hour.

Afterwards, we shared our work.

Sadie volunteered to read her piece first. Her New York moment was her trip to The Metropolitan Museum of Modern Art. Sadie began by telling us about her first trip to the MoMA with her mother, when Sadie was seven. She had been most struck by a painting by Betye Saar because the girl in its window looked like her. Sadie then wrote about seeing it again five years later, with *my* mum, on their visit to the museum earlier in the week. She described the painting in vivid detail, told us about Saar, the woman who painted it, and reflected on how, five years on, this painting and the icons that filled its window pane above the girl spoke more clearly to her than ever. It was an honest, moving and brilliant account that had Mum in tears and even made Granny, who was sitting in our lesson, stop gnawing a stick of salami to listen – high praise, indeed.

I exchanged an uneasy glance with Hussein.

'Next time, Sadie goes last,' I whispered.

Hussein was up next. His piece was on the circus. He wrote how Dmitri had made him feel welcome, entrusting him with the responsibility of Zarathustra's sound and light show and allowing him the freedom to create his own designs. Dmitri made him feel like an equal member of the Zarathustra's team, he wrote. He ended by saying the applause that rang round the Big Top on his first night was a thrill he would never forget.

It was top drawer from Hussein. Sadie and I gave him a pat on the back, Mum congratulated him and Granny thumped the floor in tribute.

Then, it was my turn.

I'd written about the Giant Taco I had for lunch at Alejandro's. A big five stars I gave it with a picture of the taco underneath.

My review drew polite applause from Hussein and Sadie and a more muted response from Mum.

Not from Granny though.

'Ho! Ho! Ho!' she chortled, slapping the table. 'I knew those flames would sizzle his brain. The boy can barely string two sentences together!'

'Hah! Shows how much you know! There are three sentences in this report,' I said smugly, parading the sheet of paper in front of her. 'Read it and weep.'

Ghost story

Max Goldman refilled his champagne glass. Shirt collar open, bow-tie undone, cigar lit, he was the picture of contentment.

'To Zarathustra's,' he cried, 'the toast of Broadway!'

'To Zarathustra's,' we chorused, tapping our water bottle and tea mug and tankard of root beer together with his champagne.

There were just the three of us left backstage

– me, Dmitri and Hussein – winding down after another rollicking show, the applause still ringing in my ears.

'Coming to New York has been very good for circus,' Dmitri confessed.

'Didn't I tell you?' Goldman bubbled. 'America loves you and the kid! Everyone is crazy about Zarathustra's.' He drained his glass and refilled it. 'Well, almost everyone. You would not believe the grief those security bozos are giving me.'

A knot of concern crossed Dmitri 's brow. 'What is the problem?'

'You're not going to believe me,' Goldman warned. 'Those knuckleheads swear their security huts are haunted. You should hear them crying into the phone to me! And all because of your fortune-teller!'

'Mathilde?' I said.

'That's the one,' Goldman fumed.

Dmitri's brow cleared. 'Mathilde . . . she can be headstrong.'

Hussein threw his head back and laughed. I nearly fell off my chair. Mathilde, headstrong? That's like saying water is wet.

Dmitri sipped his tea and insisted Goldman tell him the story.

'You like ghost stories?' Goldman said. 'Wait until you hear this one.'

It began soon after we had arrived in New York when Mathilde stopped by to visit the security guards outside Hut No. 1.

'You have disturbed zee spirits who rest here,' she told them.

The guards laughed. They weren't frightened of *spirits*. They told Mathilde to walk on and be quick about it, but, that night, the walls of their hut rattled. Its door blew open and their windows shattered.

A freak storm, they thought.

But it didn't stop.

Night after night, more odd sightings occurred: a floating jack-o-lantern, the words 'GO NOW' scratched into the panelling, a tornado of leaves – all Sadie's handiwork, of course. Listening to Max tell this ghost story, Hussein and I struggled to keep a straight face.

Desperate, the guards sought Mathilde's help to banish the spirit. Her cure, however – painting their faces red and dancing around a fire in their underwear from midnight to dawn as they chanted nursery rhymes – was only temporary. After a few days, the evil spirit returned. Worse, the spirit seemed to be spreading to the other security huts.

'No one wants to work security here any more, Dmitri!' Goldman complained. 'Word has got out that this section of Central Park is haunted. What am I going to do?'

Dmitri grinned. 'Perhaps we should employ this evil spirit.'

Guess

Each night a question about the origins of my fiery powers arrived on my phone. So far, Delilah had asked whether I:

— had been exposed to gamma rays
— had played with matches during a chemical explosion
— was a mutant in disguise
— was befriended by aliens who bestowed the gift of fire on me
— possessed a magic ring
— had drunk a witch's potion (close)
— was a distant son of the Greek god, Apollo

No, to the best of my knowledge, was my answer to the last one. The others I knocked back.

Despite being wrong, Delilah kept coming back each night for more.

I liked that.

I liked how Delilah attended each performance of Zarathustra's Travelling Circus.

I liked how she wore a Fire Boy scarf every night.

And I liked that she had promised to take me skateboarding.

As if home-schooling wasn't enough, during our second week in New York, Mum set up a live link with Miss Spatchcock's classroom. There, in all their glory, were Miss S and the rabble I'd left behind, Fink, Vialli, Jackson and Mulch sulking in the background. (It is moments like this where you find yourself wondering whether the world might be better off without the internet.)

Miss Spatchcock and the class had questions about New York ready for us: on our favourite place (Central Park); the weather (snow was in the forecast); the subway (we hadn't been on it yet); the pizza (amazing, and sold by the slice); who the girl in the room was and why she was sitting so close to me (nice try, Fink); whether we'd seen any film stars (yes) and lots more.

Miss Spatchcock moved the questioning on to

the day's topic – Fire Boy in America. *The Caversham Chronicle* intended to run a front-page story on how New Yorkers had welcomed Fire Boy and Zarathustra's Travelling Circus. 'With open arms,' I had planned on telling them.

Until I read the morning edition of New York's *Daily Herald*, that is. Delilah wasn't the only one who wanted to play Guess, it seemed.

GIVE **FIRE BOY** A
COLD SHOWER!
TELL THE *HERALD*
HOW HE FLIES
AND **WIN $10,000!**

Underneath they printed a photo of me blazing through the air. The caption read: **EXPOSE THE FAKE**.

The article said:

Who is this flaming nuisance? Is he real? Does he have a name or is it a special-effects wind-up? The *Herald* wants to know! That's why we are offering readers $10,000 for any information leading to the unmasking of Fire Boy. New Yorkers deserve to know the TRUTH. Join the *Herald*'s campaign and we'll send Fire Boy packing!

Reward money for information on me and my powers?

I was not pleased. Neither were Mum or Dmitri.

No one wanted spies outside our windows or long-lens cameras trained on our caravans. Maybe our haunting of Leviathan's security team had been too hasty. Right now, I wouldn't mind seeing those lads patrolling our fence and scaring away fortune-seekers.

My one consolation was that Miss Spatchcock and her class knew nothing about the *Herald*. It was a New York paper and wasn't printed in Britain.

Miss Spatchcock told me Joe Jackson had a question.

'Hello, Sweeney,' Jackson said. 'Have you ever heard of a paper called the *Daily Herald*? This morning, Mulch emailed us a link to an article in it.'

This struck me as an ideal time to sever our connection. Needing a little computo-power, I made eyes at Hussein. 'What do you think, mate? Are we buffering? I think we're losing them.'

Mum leaned in. 'Take your hands away from the keyboard, Hussein.' To me she snapped, 'I know what you're trying to do. Answer the question. There's nothing wrong with this connection.'

I unmuted myself. 'I'm afraid I don't read the *Daily Herald*, Jackson. I don't know what you're talking about.'

'Do you mean this *Daily Herald*?' cackled Granny. She tossed the paper on to my keyboard. 'They're offering reward money for information on Fire Boy.'

I glared at the old witch. 'Gee, thanks. Everyone is being SO helpful this morning.'

'That's the paper I mean,' Jackson said, unmuting himself. Lowering his voice, he winked into the camera. 'Come on, Sweeney. You and I have been down this road before. Spill the beans. Tell us who Fire Boy is and how he makes his fire. Let's be the first to print it. Then you and I can split the money.'

Fink elbowed her way forward. 'You said we'd all get a cut!'

'Don't worry, Fink,' Jackson grunted. 'You'll get your sniff.'

Vialli shouldered herself into the picture. 'Do it for Miss Spatchcock, Sweeney! Tell us first! Let the school paper print it! I'll write it for you!' she screeched. 'Revealing Fire Boy's identity can be our world exclusive!'

'Back in your box, glory-hound!' spat Fink. 'I'll write the exclusive. It was my idea!'

'Write? Hah! I don't think you can!' Vialli volleyed back. 'All you're good for is inventing sordid little rumours!'

'Says who?' screeched Fink.

'Says me!' stormed Vialli.

Back in Miss Spatchcock's classroom, a small tussle broke out.

Granny flicked the ashes of her black cigar into a teacup. 'They should give this lot a spot on daytime television. I'd watch them each morning.'

Despite the lads in the back row egging them on, Fink vs. Vialli promised more than it delivered. Miss Spatchcock was quick to separate the girls and by then Fink was already backing down (Vialli was captain of the girls' hockey team and would have wiped the floor with her). As the others shouted and pushed and squawked and shoved, a lone figure climbed on to his chair and pointed a finger at the screen.

It was Mulch.

'I know who Fire Boy is,' he growled. 'I saw him hiding inside the vaulting box the first night he appeared. I've always known.'

Sadie and Hussein shot me a frightened glance. Oh, well. I always knew this day was coming. If anything, I was surprised Mulch had waited this long. For once, he was telling the truth. Mulch *had* seen me inside the vaulting box on the night Fire Boy was born. He *had* seen me ignite.

Every head in the classroom turned towards him.

Staring me in the eyes – well, as best you can from a few thousand miles away – he pointed his finger and declared, 'Fire Boy is . . . AIDAN SWEENEY!'

The classroom fell silent.

So did the caravan.

Mum froze.

Sadie and Hussein held their breath.

Granny belched and a feather of smoke escaped my nether regions.

And then the classroom erupted.

Children roared with laughter. They banged their desks. They slapped their chairs. They hooted and howled.

No one could believe I was Fire Boy.

'Sweeney? Fly?' laughed Jackson.

'Aidan Sweeney on *fire*?' mocked Fink.

'Aidan?' giggled Miss Spatchcock. 'Really, Mitchell! I never realised you had such a fanciful imagination!'

A lifetime of mishaps – walking into a closed door and breaking my nose (aged 8); an inability to remember my times tables (ongoing); locking myself in the games cupboard (aged 10); entering an assembly without my kit on (last month); and more, much more – left me free from suspicion. No one could believe that I might be the all-conquering, all-powerful Fire Boy. Which hurt a little. Still, it did mean that my secret identity was safe – much to Mulch's horror.

Mulch (insert peals of laughter here) did not take it well.

He fumed. He swore. He stomped around the room shouting at everyone to stop laughing, which of course only made them guffaw louder. His failed attempt at outing me seemed to drive him to the very brink. Hopping off his chair, he pushed his way to the front until his nasty face filled the screen.

'I fly to New York tomorrow, Sweeney,' Mulch sneered into the camera, 'and I swear that I won't rest until the whole world knows who you are!'

trust me

I slid out of bed, easing down the edge so as not to wake Hussein. A mid-morning splash of sunlight poured through a porthole window.

I strolled to the other end of the caravan. Sadie was there, her long legs draped over an armchair, a book in her hands and Lemon napping in her lap.

I said, 'I feel like pancakes. *American* pancakes.'

Sadie closed her book. 'I am always up for pancakes.'

From somewhere upstairs Mum called out, 'There are blueberries in the refrigerator we need to use.'

Reader, my mother.

Badger her with requests to her face and she can't hear you. Make a comment to someone else on another floor and she is sensitive to variations of pitch at distances that would shame a German Shepherd.

'Can you manage or shall I come down?' Mum shouted.

The frying pan rose from the top of the stove and flew into Sadie's hand. 'We got this,' she said.

Lemon raised her head from Sadie's lap and blinked at the frying pan.

'We'll be fine!' I yelled at the ceiling.

The refrigerator opened. Out came a jug of milk. Then the eggs popped out of their packet and bobbed through the air. One by one, they dived, cracking their shells against a bowl and dropping their yokes inside.

Lemon, wide awake now, sprang to the countertop and stared into the bowl.

'Away you,' I said, getting out the flour and mixing bowl. While Sadie measured the flour and milk, I woke Hussein. If we wanted the ultimate in smooth batter, we needed his electro-touch to push the blender up a notch or two.

It didn't take him long to get the batter whizzing. When he was finished, Sadie added the blueberries.

I ignited my hand and heated the frying pan.

We were ready.

We took turns pouring different-sized pancakes.

I heated the skillet and, when they browned, Sadie flipped them. Round the room pancakes spun like little frisbees. Lemon made us laugh as she tried to stalk them, leaping at the pancakes as they flew by, so we made a tiny bird-shaped one just for her.

Hussein laid the table. I got out the maple syrup and the cream Hussein had whipped and soon all of us – Mum and Granny too – were sitting down to a feast.

Afterwards, Sadie FaceTimed Mimi, Hussein strummed his guitar, Granny sat down to watch an episode of Ultimate Cage Fighting Volume IV and I helped Mum wash up.

It was bliss.

A perfect morning with Sadie, Hussein, Lemon and Mum. Granny too.

And then Sloane Sixsmith messaged me. Life was never the same after that.

The media buzzed around the circus after the *Daily Herald* piece. Reporters badgered Dmitri for statements on Fire Boy and demanded an interview. Like the cavalry, Max Goldman arrived to bat these questions away. For Goldman, the *Herald* article was free publicity, an opportunity for him to shift more Fire Boy merchandise. That afternoon he held a press conference outside the Big Top and addressed the accusation that Fire Boy was a fake.

'You want answers? Read the programme!' Goldman quipped, holding up a copy.

A reporter said, 'Zarathustra's Travelling Circus claims that Fire Boy is a demon and over a thousand years old. Are you saying that's true?'

Goldman's eyes widened. 'Of course, I am!' he cried as if he could not believe anyone would doubt him. 'That's why the *Herald* is picking on him!' The demon community, Goldman explained, had gotten a lot of bad press over the years. 'I admit, some of it deserved,' he said, holding his hands up. But now it was time to move forward. 'Fire Boy,' Goldman trumpeted, 'is a fiery beacon for change, an inspiration for demons everywhere.' It was pure bravado, a tongue-in-cheek performance, a light-hearted way of stonewalling questions about my identity and defusing the *Herald* article.

It worked, more or less.

#WhoisFireBoy stopped trending online. The

rows of photographers positioned outside the fence and in the trees drifted away. The traffic on the @fireboy page slowed.

Most of it, anyway.

After chatting with Mimi, Sadie spent the morning on the Fire Boy Instagram. She posted two photos of me on fire and was working her way through the comments when she came across a direct message request from an account called @thesloanesixsmith.

'*The* Sloane Sixsmith?' she read aloud. 'No. It can't be.'

'What are the chances?' I said, peeking over her shoulder.

'Check her profile,' Hussein said, squeezing on the sofa for a look.

There wasn't much to see. The @thesloanesixsmith profile had one post (a photo of rolling green hills and hedge fences) and no followers.

Hussein said, 'Let's see which accounts she's following.'

The Fire Boy account was top of @thesloane sixsmith's list. Underneath it were organisations like Friends of the Earth, Green Life, Save our

Oceans and people like Greta Thunberg and David Attenborough.

'Shall I accept her message?' Sadie asked.

'Go ahead,' I said. 'If it's her, we ought to know.'

'Are you sure?' Hussein asked nervously.

'Yeah,' I drawled. 'How bad can it be?'

Sadie clicked the paper plane icon and a video appeared in the message box.

We pushed play.

Surprise.

It was Sloane Sixsmith.

Hello, Aidan. I love what you're doing with Fire Boy. The flying. The flames and fireworks. I'm a big fan. I'm coming to New York soon and can't wait to see you in person.

Oh, fudge.

I don't need to introduce myself, do I? I know MI5 sent you my video. Funny, isn't it, how our paths keep crossing? You and I have never met, yet we seem linked together. It must be fate.

'How can she know we've seen the video?' Sadie asked.

Hussein frowned. 'A hunch, maybe? The link MI5 sent was untraceable. There's no way Sloane could know whether we watched it.'

I flew into London last week. It was the first time I've been back in years. So much has changed. Still, I'm glad I came. It gave me a chance to meet a friend of yours.

Sloane's face began to lengthen. Her nose flattened and stretched. The mousey-brown hair that hung to her shoulders shortened. Her eyes went brown. Her skin darkened. Tiny hairs sprouted on her chin and lip.

'No. No. No. No,' wailed Hussein.

'Oh, please. Not him,' Sadie moaned. 'Not him.'

Me? I was too stunned to speak. Because the person on the screen gazing back at us was no longer Sloane Sixsmith. It was Agent Whittaker.

Russell is very fond of you, Aidan. The circus too,

but he's most worried about what might happen to you.

As am I.

It was uncanny. Sloane had the same gravelly voice as Agent Whittaker. The same pitch and accent. The same jaded expression. All she needed was the navy suit and pink tie.

You and the circus are exposed in New York, Aidan. You see, no one paid Fire Boy much attention at first. You were a novelty, a circus act. That's not true now. People are taking an interest in Fire Boy – people in power. The type of people who will let nothing stand in their way when they want something.

Nothing.

Lemon, it seemed, had climbed on to the back of the chair while I was glued to Sloane's video. She picked this very moment to leap on to my shoulder.

Did I scream?

You bet I did.

There is a way to stop these people though. You and I can do it together.

Sloane's face began to change.

Her skin became lighter. Her hair lengthened. Her goatee disappeared and her eyes reverted to their hazel brown.

But there's one thing you must do first.

Destroy the serum.

Destroy the jar of Nature's Own now, Aidan, before it's too late. It is far too powerful. We cannot take the chance that it will fall into the wrong hands. And it will if we're not careful.

Please, trust me. I will explain why when I see you. Until then, stay safe.

The video ended there.

the secret keeper

We watched the video three times, not that it helped. If anything, it left us with more questions.

Sadie, Hussein and I had assumed Sloane wanted the jar of sweets back because they were worth so much money. Agent Whittaker – the *real* Agent Whittaker – had presumed the same. Yet here was Sloane urging me to destroy the last drops of the serum *she* had prepared . . .

Why?

The three of us struggled to get our heads around it. Why would Sloane want to destroy the serum she had created? It was a miracle, truly one of its kind. If we got rid of it, the world would never see the likes of it again.

As for trusting Sloane . . . that was a big ask.

'Don't even think about it,' Hussein scowled. 'Destroying the sweets doesn't sound rational to me. You'd be mad to listen to her.'

Sadie agreed. 'There's no way we can tell whether Sloane's telling the truth – or all of it, anyway. She never mentioned me or Hussein, did she?'

No.

She hadn't.

Hussein's chin wobbled. He took his glasses off and cleaned them, avoiding our eyes. 'Sloane must know about us – *all* of us now. She must. She'll know everything that was in Agent Whittaker's head.'

Did she?

Could Sloane flick through a person's memory as if it were a book and pick out the significant events with a yellow highlighter?

Would one's memory come with an index where passwords, phone numbers, addresses, the names of the planets and who won the FA Cup last year are filed alphabetically?

Sadie shuddered. 'Dmitri was right. Sloane's powers *are* scary.'

Dmitri.

His name alone gave me hope. If anyone could see a way through this, it was him. Only there was something I had to do first.

Alone.

But before I could move, my phone buzzed.

A text message sent from Delilah Jones to Aidan Sweeney at 12:15pm:

You had better not have forgotten what today is . . .

A text message sent from Aidan Sweeney to Delilah Jones at 12:16pm:

Thursday?

A text message sent from Delilah Jones to Aidan Sweeney at 12:16pm:

A text message sent from Delilah Jones to Aidan Sweeney at 12:16pm:

You're meeting my granddaddy TODAY!!! Remember?

A text message sent from Delilah Jones to Aidan Sweeney at 12:16pm:

A car will pick you up at 2 from the circus. Granddaddy can't wait to meet you! 🔥

'That was Delilah. I nearly forgot. I'm meeting her grandfather today.'

Sadie made a face. 'My! Things are moving fast! Invited over to meet the parents already, are we?'

'Shut up.'

Hussein picked his coat off the chair and began moving to the door. 'Let's go. We can't wait any longer. We need to tell Dmitri that Sloane is on her way.'

'He'll need to contact Agent Whittaker too,' Sadie said. She stopped and looked back at me.

I had remained rooted to the chair.

'Are you coming?'

'You two go on ahead,' I said. 'There's something I need to do first.'

Sadie eyed me suspiciously. 'Don't be long,' she said at last.

I waited until they were outside before getting down on my knees. I pulled out the suitcase which

I kept hidden under the sofa and rifled through my winter clothes searching for a very particular sock.

The one with the jar of Nature's Own inside it.

Four phrases (in no particular order) that best describe the contents of my jar of Nature's Own:

- Formerly ten (now four) jellied mints from the cloud forests of Peru, dusted with frosting sugar and covered with liquorice laces
- Formerly ten (now four) nut-sized capsules of a fruit-juice-based serum from *el Árbol de los Dioses*, the sacred tree of the Ancient Incas, hidden inside each mint
- The delicious source of my powers; survivors of fire-bombs on two different continents
- The most valuable jar of sweets in the world

I removed the sock.

I slid the jar out and held it in my hands.

When we lived in London, I used to take the jar out most nights before I went to sleep. I liked to check the sweets were safe, and sniff the peppermint scent that still wafted out whenever I opened the jar. I had got out of the habit in New York.

When Sadie returned the jar to me after we landed, I had put it in my sock drawer and tried not to disturb it.

I opened the jar and counted the sweets. All four were inside.

I rolled one of them between my thumb and forefinger, examining its liquorice laces and powdered jelly. The urge to devour it was overwhelming.

Destroy these sweets?

NO WAY.

Lemon nosed forwards, brushing under my arm. Her whiskers twitched.

'Forget it,' I said, dropping the sweet back into the jar and resealing its lid. 'You're powerful enough.'

I ran to Mathilde's caravan.

'Mathilde!' I shouted, banging on the door to her caravan. 'Let me in!'

'What do you want?' Mathilde snapped when she saw me. She had her earphones in and white, paint-splattered overalls on.

'Can I come in?' I asked. 'It's important.'

Mathilde studied me closely. I felt like a tarot

card – the Fool, she'd say – as I stood in the doorway waiting for her to divine my intentions. 'Enter,' she said, 'but touch nothing and ask no questions.'

Lemon snuck past as Mathilde led me inside. Climbing into a leather armchair near the window, she circled the cushion twice and lay down.

I peered into the dimly lit room. A drop cloth was thrown over the middle of the floor. An easel stood in its centre. Beside it was a small round table. Long brushes and a palette smeared with swirls of red and orange sat on it. Canvases of street scenes were pinned to the wall. One showed a building on fire with two people emerging from its lobby.

'What are you painting?' I asked.

'No questions,' Mathilde said sternly, turning me round so I faced her. 'What do you want?'

I told her about Sloane and described the video she'd posted, how she transformed into Agent Whittaker and told me to destroy the jar of Nature's Own.

'I need a favour.'

'If it is a tarot reading, I cannot help,' Mathilde shrugged. 'Zis shape-shifter has too many faces. I cannot see her in zee cards. One days she is zee

Queen of Cups, the next a Page.'

'I don't want my fortune read.' I removed the jar of Nature's Own from my pocket. 'I was hoping you would look after this for me.'

Mathilde held the jar as if it were a glass bee's nest, peering eagerly inside it, wary of disturbing the forces within.

'Don't tell me where you hide it,' I said. 'Just take it. If Sloane is in New York, it's not safe in my hands.'

'You do not want to destroy zee sweets?' Mathilde asked.

'No,' I answered. 'Powers can be used for good too. I know that might sound crazy when you look at the world today, but I believe they can.'

Mathilde arched a studded eyebrow. 'And who will stop me from taking one of zee sweets if you give zee jar to me?'

'No one.'

She smirked. In her black lipstick, her mouth looked like a lopsided comma. 'You trust me?'

'Yes.'

Mathilde gazed back at me tenderly, like Mum does when I show her a bruise I've picked up playing football. 'Be careful, little Fool. Our hearts can often lead us astray. But I shall accept your request and be your secret keeper.'

Mathilde held her right hand up and spat into it, a right gobber too. 'Shake.'

I stared at her spit-stained palm. 'Seriously?'

Mathilde nodded.

I shook her hand, only to discover I was supposed to spit in my hand first, so we had to start again.

Yuk.

It was what you might call a sticky encounter.

The Rolls Royce – a very nice ride, by the way, should a billionaire ever send one to pick you up; beats an Uber hands-down – stopped in front of Frontier Towers on 57th Street, a tall skyscraper with views over Central Park. The entire lobby was glass-fronted and was a city-block wide, i.e. huge. Enormous screens set inside the windows faced outwards, broadcasting live coverage from *Frontier News*, Frontier's Cartoon Network and trailers from upcoming Frontier Films.

Dead-Eye Dolores stamped her boots and waved her cowboy hat. 'Yeehaw! Look at that, will ya? I ain't never been to a billionaire's house before!'

Did I mention that Dead-Eye was with me?

Dead-Eye was with me.

Once Dmitri saw Sloane's video message, Operation Lock, Stock and Shock went into high alert status. No one could leave the circus grounds without a partner and even inside we were encouraged to buddy-up. When I said Delilah was expecting me, Mum had offered to tag along – 'I can't think of anything I'd enjoy more than watching my son and Delilah all afternoon' were her exact words – but Dmitri (thank God) had opted for the gunslinger.

A good choice Dead-Eye was too. Easy-going. Nerves of steel.

The same could not be said for the rest of the circus. Sloane masquerading as Agent Whittaker had spooked us all. Dmitri had rung him straight away with links to the video. Agent Whittaker called it a major security breach and had the video removed from Instagram immediately. The likelihood of Sloane coming to New York meant Agent Whittaker had to contact his counterparts in the US. He promised to stay in touch with us over the next few days or until Sloane made contact.

Delilah took Dead-Eye joining us in her stride. True, Delilah did get a fright when she entered the lobby and saw everyone on the floor except Dead-Eye and three security guards in a face-off (they had tried to get her to remove her six-guns) but Delilah was able to defuse the situation quickly. As she said, 'There are some advantages to being the boss's granddaughter.'

We followed Delilah into the Tower's private elevator. To open its doors, you needed eye, voice *and* handprint verification. 'Hot damn!' cried Dead-Eye. 'This is like being in a Bond film.'

It was a long ride to the top.

'I'm sorry to hear your grandpappy's been poorly, Miss Delilah,' Dead-Eye said. 'If there's anything I can do, you just let me know.'

Delilah squeezed my hand. 'I think the best cure for my granddaddy is the boy standing right next to you, Dolores.'

'Aidan?' Dead-Eye guffawed. 'That boy couldn't cure a ham. Unlessin' you planning on giving the old fella a heat massage, that is. I reckon he'd be good at that.'

I thanked Dead-Eye for the vote of confidence.

When we reached the 90th floor, the lift stopped. We emerged into a room that was wider than a football pitch and so tall that I almost felt like I was back in the Big Top.

'Granddaddy calls this his Trophy Room,' Delilah explained.

A brief list (in no particular order) of items on display in Clayton Jones's Trophy Room:

- Photographs of Clayton Jones alongside presidents, prime ministers, kings, queens and famous sporting personalities
- A stuffed grizzly bear standing three metres tall
- A gun collection comprised of historic relics (a musket used during the War of Independence), military firearms (a Thompson submachine gun), classics (a Colt .45 and a Winchester rifle) and much more
- Framed magazines like *Time*, *Fortune*, *Vanity Fair* and others, all featuring Clayton Jones on their covers
- A map of the world highlighting Frontier News and Media outlets
- A silk-screen painting of Clayton Jones by Andy Warhol

When Dead-Eye saw the gun case, she clicked her heels and whooped. Like a four year old with her nose pressed against the window of a sweet shop, she stared at Clayton Jones's collection with awe and envy.

I fought the urge to do the same with the views from the windows. We were so high up I was afraid I might ignite like I had in the plane when I saw the clouds outside. I didn't get the feeling Clayton Jones would be too impressed if I burnt down his Trophy Room.

Delilah interrupted our trophy-gazing. 'Dead-Eye, I'm afraid I'm going to have to ask you to wait here. Is that all right? The doctor said we ought to limit how many visitors my granddaddy gets until he's back on his feet again.'

Dead-Eye waved her cowboy hat in the air. 'You young 'uns enjoy yourselves. I'll be mighty fine right here.'

We took a left at the grizzly bear and walked down a long hallway. On the way we passed a medieval suit of armour, two samurai swords and a crossbow.

'Any burglar who breaks into this apartment is in for a nasty surprise,' I said.

'That's nothing,' Delilah said. 'Wait until you see

the guillotine and electric chair.'

'The *what*?' I cried.

'Joke,' Delilah smirked. Linking her arm in mine, she led me to the foot of a staircase. From above us came the sounds of a one-sided argument, as if someone were shouting into a phone.

Delilah rolled her eyes. 'That must be Granddaddy's TV. Because his hearing is going, he turns the volume up so high you need earplugs to be in the same room.'

'Tell me about it,' I laughed. 'The walls shake when my Granny watches TV.'

Delilah started climbing the stairs. 'I'm going to tell him you're here. While I'm gone, why don't you wash your hands. Until my granddaddy's a bit better, we're trying to keep his room as germ-free as we can.'

I tried to follow Delilah's directions to the bathroom, but ended up in a fitness studio. Mirrors ran along one wall. Racks of weights were at one end, parallel bars at another. Cardio machines – rowers, StairMasters, treadmills, stationary bikes – were placed at measured intervals. What really caught my attention though, were the posters.

Framed life-size posters of Captain Marvel, Cat Woman, Harley Quinn, Poison Ivy and Dark Phoenix decorated the walls. I was having a go at the rowing machine when Delilah walked in.

'There you are!' she cried. 'I was wondering where you had wandered off to.'

'Nice gym,' I said. 'Is this yours?'

'Yes,' she replied.

'The posters too?'

'Yes,' Delilah said, colouring slightly.

I jerked my thumb at the poster of Harley Quinn. She had a baseball bat in one hand and a pistol in the other. 'Does it bother you that so many of them are villains?'

Delilah shrugged. 'I prefer to think of them as strong, independent-minded women.'

Clayton Jones was sitting up in bed. His white hair was uncombed and sprouted unevenly in small patches. A pair of reading glasses hung from his neck and he had navy pyjamas on. For a man confined to bed, he was in good nick. He retained a tan, seemed lively and certainly looked like he hadn't lost his appetite. Phones, a laptop, folders and newspapers were scattered on the sheets. Around the bed were a drip, a heart monitor and a machine on a trolley that went *bing* every few seconds.

The rest of his bedroom resembled an office on the floor of the New York Stock Exchange. Two walls were filled with wide-screen televisions broadcasting news reports from all over the globe. Images of newscasters, weather forecasts, stock market reports, floods and grinning presidents bombarded my eyes. It was hard to know where to look. How anyone could make sense of these multi-screens with the sound on (Delilah had turned it off when we entered) was beyond me.

Above his bed was a photo that had been enlarged into a canvas. Taken at sea, it showed Clayton Jones in sunglasses and a sailing jacket, aboard a yacht. He was at the helm, the wind lashing his hair. Delilah, who looked as though she'd been about eight at the time, stood next to him, one hand on the ship's wheel.

Clayton Jones motioned to the chair beside his bed and told me to sit down.

'I must thank you, young man,' he began. 'You and your circus have put a smile on my granddaughter's face again, and for that I will be forever in your debt.'

I thanked him for bringing me and Zarathustra's to New York. 'If it weren't for you and Delilah, I'd be in school right now and Dmitri would be on his way to Scotland. You don't owe me anything.'

Delilah turned to me. 'Aidan, could you show my granddaddy your flames? He would love to see them up-close. And don't worry! I had a word with the doctor. He said a few flames won't cause any damage in here.'

I rolled up my sleeves and for the next half-hour I flamed on and off. I answered questions about the heat I could generate, side effects, whether I was thirsty afterwards, changes to my appetite and flying – lots about flying.

Clayton Jones reached towards me and warmed his hands against my fire. His face glowed. I could see tiny flames – my flames – shining in his eyes and Delilah's. 'Extraordinary,' he murmured.

I extinguished my flames.

The old man straightened his sheets and tutted. 'You are a living wonder, Aidan Sweeney. I have seen many strange sights in this old world, but nothing like that.' He let out a contented sigh and folded his hands over his chest. 'Delilah, would you very much mind if I had a moment alone with your young friend? We need to have a man-to-man talk.'

'Man-to-man?' Delilah mocked, rolling her eyes. 'I might just want to stick around for that one.'

I wouldn't if I were her. Manly chats in my experience – visits to see the Head, mostly

– consisted of long sermons on discipline and my lack of it.

The billionaire overruled his granddaughter. 'Never you mind, Delilah,' he said. 'You wait outside. I will bring Aidan out shortly.'

Clayton Jones waited until the door closed. Then he addressed me.

'Aidan, my granddaughter means the world to me. Delilah is all I have and I want her to be happy. You understand that, don't you?'

'Yes, sir,' I replied.

'Good. Because there is something Delilah wants, something she wants more than anything in the world.'

The old man's dark eyes darted over me. He straightened his shoulders and winked. 'I bet you already know what I'm going to say.'

I did.

'Delilah wants a superpower. Can you help her?'

I said nothing.

'It was never a real problem until you came along. A bit of fantasy, dressing up on Halloween, a comic book addiction. Visits to the cinema to see *Black Panther* and *The Avengers*. Nothing out of the ordinary. Until Fire Boy showed up, no one imagined superpowers could be real. But now Delilah knows it's possible.'

I stared at my shoes.

It wasn't the first time in the last three weeks that I had toyed with the idea of surprising Delilah with a minty sweet.

Did I dare?

Was Delilah that much different than Sadie, Hussein and me? I didn't think so.

I couldn't see anyone – Sadie, Hussein, Mum, Dmitri or Mathilde – approving, but none of them knew Delilah as well as I did. Getting the sweets back off Mathilde might not be easy, but I didn't think she'd say no.

And just like that, I decided.

Delilah would be one of us. The gang of four – me, Sadie, Hussein and Lemon – would soon become five.

Rule #23 from *The BIG BOOK of Superheroes*:

Never be afraid to extend an arm of friendship. Two superheroes working alone are no match for two superheroes working together.

Luck had favoured me when the jar of Nature's Own landed in my lap. Why shouldn't it favour Delilah as well – and in double-quick time too, before Sloane Sixsmith showed up and put an end to them.

'Leave it with me, Mr Jones,' I said, raising my head. 'I'll see what I can do.'

The old man reached over and patted my head like I was a retriever. 'Good boy! I knew I could count on you. I will, of course, reimburse you handsomely for—'

I stopped him. 'I don't want any money.'

'People always say that, Aidan,' Clayton Jones chortled, 'and they always regret it. What *is* important is that you and I have an understanding. Both of us want what's best for Delilah, don't we?'

I nodded my head.

'Just do me one favour, will you, son? Before you give Delilah this potion or pill, you let me see it first. I want to be in the room when her big moment comes. It would mean so much to me.'

'Sure, Mr Jones,' I said. 'I won't hand anything over to Delilah without letting you know.'

'Good boy! Now fetch me my cane. We don't

want Delilah to start worrying.'

While Clayton Jones struggled out of bed and on to his feet, I helped him with his slippers and gave him his cane.

Slowly, we made our way towards the steps. As we walked, Clayton Jones chatted about London. He owned a house in Mayfair and a castle in York. 'You must come and visit us there,' he said.

I told him I'd like that.

He shuffled down the steps one at a time, gripping the bannister tightly. 'I'm not long off the phone with one of my London editors, in fact. Strange tidings. Strange tidings, indeed,' he huffed.

I smiled at Delilah who was waiting for us at the bottom of the stairs.

'Rumours of an infiltrator at MI5,' he continued, 'a shape-shifter, whatever that means. The security forces are in a flutter about it I'm told.'

I froze. 'A shape-shifter?'

'I know,' the old man chuckled. 'Sounds like some kind of wizard, doesn't it? Whoever this "shape-shifter" is, he's flying into New York today. I expect Homeland Patrol already has him behind bars. The fool! Why would he step on to a plane?

Didn't he know Homeland Patrol would be waiting for him when he landed?'

So it was happening.

Sloane Sixsmith was arriving in New York.

Today.

'Aidan! What's wrong?' Delilah cried. 'You look like you've seen a ghost!'

It felt like I had.

No one could stop Sloane Sixsmith.

The authorities in South America failed and so had Agent Whittaker and MI5. What chance did Homeland Patrol have?

What chance did *I* have?

I sat down on the steps right there and then and texted Mum, Sadie and Hussein. I told them what Clayton Jones had said about Sloane.

Delilah told her grandfather to go to the Trophy Room and entertain Dead-Eye – 'Talk guns with her. That's all you gotta do!' – and took me by the hand. She led me to an antique, two-seater settee where we could be alone. 'Aidan, I want you to tell me what's troubling you. I can't help if you don't.'

So I started talking.

Sloane. The jar of Nature's Own. Everything.

Once I uncorked that bottle inside me, it all poured out.

And Delilah listened, wide-eyed and with bated breath.

So I kept talking.

countdown

6:15pm

Entered the Big Top in full Fire Boy regalia. Superman – if you believe what you read in the comics – can fly to the moon at a moment's notice. Good on him, I say. Not me though. If I wanted to achieve maximum heat later on, I needed to rekindle the flames with a pre-performance dress rehearsal. Here in the real world, superheroes loosen up before a gig.

I walked to centre ring and ignited. I ascended slowly and began with a few laps over the empty stands. On the fifth go-round, I picked up the pace. Faster and faster I flew until I was an orange-and-red blur.

Loved that.

Spins, nose-dives and loop-the-loops came next. After completing my last somersault, I rehearsed the 'extras': the fireballs I aimed at the scorched earth mark on the left of the centre ring; popped fire-bangers (fistfuls of flames that explode) and cracked off fire-sparkles (flecks of flames that spiral into the air before fading); and finished up with some fiery sprints across the Big Top.

It felt good to burn again. I needed to clear my head.

When I returned to the dressing room, I placed my costume on its peg and checked that my snack pack (Extra Spicy Corn Crisps, two chocolate bars, water bottle) was full.

A true professional leaves nothing to chance.

6:45pm

Met Sadie and Hussein at the merchandise stall. Sadie sported a Zarathustra's Travelling Circus jersey (maroon with gold lettering), a Fire Boy beanie and a necklace of Zarathustra's pins attached to a ribbon. Hussein had on a Fire Boy scarf. Somewhere, I expect, Max Goldman was puffing on a cigar and grinning.

Both of them, I noticed, had gloves on. As a defence against skin-on-skin contact with Sloane

Sixsmith and her powers, gloves didn't offer much protection, but they were the best we could do. Hussein and I had considered covering ourselves in bubble wrap from head to toe until Sadie pointed out that a) it might draw attention and b) breathing might prove difficult.

So gloves it was.

A sudden blast of wind whistled through Central Park. Cold and bitter, it shook the stall. Scarves flapped, balloons shivered on their sticks and the fiery-red T-shirts shuddered. Two Fire Boy action figures wobbled off the shelf and fell.

I bent down to pick them up.

The arm of Flyer had snapped off and Smokey's head had rolled into a puddle.

Ouch.

I was never one for omens, but seeing your action figure replicas in bits can put a person off.

6:50pm

Organ music boomed out the speakers. *Bumpetty ba bump! Bumpetty ba bump! Ba ba bah!*

The carousel stirred into life.

The circus gates opened and ticket holders

steamed forwards, taking their seats in the Big Top.

Max Goldman watched them arrive. Leaning back in his box seat, he lit a cigar. 'Kid, my phone has not stopped ringing this week. Do you know why?'

'Andrew wasn't there to answer it?' I chanced.

'Mr Goldman's phone and I do not part,' Andrew corrected. 'I maintain contact with it at all times.'

Goldman blew a smoke ring into the air. 'My phone keeps ringing because people want to talk about *you*,' he said.

'Me?'

'You,' Goldman gloated.

Andrew nodded his head. 'It's true,' he mouthed.

'Film producers, publishers, New York's Fire Department, children's TV, Doritos – everyone wants a piece of you.'

'Doritos?' I said casually.

Goldman popped his cigar out his mouth and grinned at me. 'They're talking about putting out an Extra-Intense Flaming-Hot Corn Crisp and they want *you* on the packet.'

I took a deep breath to steady myself, then asked, 'If I agree to this deal, I get free Doritos, don't I?'

'By the truckload, kid,' Goldman replied.

This. Was. The. Dream.

'You and I will get together after the show,' Goldman beamed. 'We have a lot to talk about.'

7:30pm

'It is time,' Dmitri said, opening the dressing room door. 'Good luck, everyone!' Decked out in his red ringmaster's suit and black top hat, he stepped out into the entrance tunnel.

The cast followed.

The Red Arrows marched in perfect formation. Eshe and Rodrigo twirled by. Head held high, a haughty Mathilde strode into the corridor. The Kerrigans jostled into position in their huge Krazy Klown shoes. Atlas – shirtless (T-shirt number one of the evening hadn't made it past the door) – glistened with oil. Dead-Eye loped by, a six-gun in each hand. Gareth the magician ambled out and Gladys the Wonder Dog, her nose in the air, trotted after him. Kenise came last, sleek and powerful in her cat-like black tights.

I locked the door to the dressing room after they left. I had a few minutes before my grand entrance.

Fire Boy entered the arena last by zooming over everyone's heads, the red-hot cherry on top of the opening sequence. Flicking the monitor on, I watched them walk in and waited for my cue.

Maybe that's why I never heard the latch click.

The dressing room door swung open. Instantly, I ignited from the neck up, hiding my face behind the flames.

'Aidan! I had to see you.'

It was Delilah. 'How did you get backstage?' I said, extinguishing my flames.

'Max let me in. I wanted to speak with you. My granddaddy showed me the video Sloane Sixsmith posted.'

'How?' I asked. 'MI5 pulled that down.'

'When you're as rich as my grandfather is, it's easy to pull a few strings. Aidan, I heard her lies and saw what that shape-shifter can do. You and I need to put an end to her.'

'An *end*?' I squeaked.

'A once-and-for-all end,' Delilah said fiercely.

'You mean . . .'

'Burn her. Turn your flames on her. Rid the world of Sloane Sixsmith before she steals those sweets and becomes too powerful to defeat.'

'I couldn't do that,' I protested.

'You can and you will, Aidan,' Delilah insisted. 'It's what superheroes do. I don't believe for one minute that Sloane wants to destroy that jar. She wants those sweets for herself. The only thing she intends to destroy is you!'

'ME?'

'Yes, you,' Delilah snorted. 'Some people don't care who they gotta step on to get what they want.'

I shook my head.

'I don't know, Delilah. I don't think I can burn another person.'

Delilah gazed up at me with big blue eyes and sighed. 'Aidan Sweeney, you are too sweet for words. I knew you'd say that. I even said it to my Granddaddy before I came here. I said, *That boy wouldn't hurt a fly*.'

'You did?'

'I did,' Delilah said. 'That's why I want you to tell me where you're hiding those sweets. You give me one now and I can help you.'

'Help me?'

'That's right.' Delilah edged nearer. 'If I had

superpowers, you and I could be a team. And Aidan? This girl would have no problem burning that shape-shifter to the ground, you know what I'm sayin'?'

I nodded my head.

'Good,' Delilah purred. 'Now, *where* are you hiding those sweets?'

'Delilah,' I said, checking the monitor over her head, 'I've got to go.'

'No, you don't,' she insisted. 'People are late all the time. The circus can wait. You and I have to sort this out first.'

'But I can't wait,' I said anxiously, glancing again at Dmitri on the monitor. 'That's my cue.'

Delilah slapped a palm on my chest, stopping me in my tracks. 'Aidan Sweeney, don't you DARE walk out on me!'

'I–I–I've got to go!' I cried, sidestepping her and racing out the door.

The last sound I heard before I ignited and lifted off was Delilah warning me that I'd regret choosing the circus over her.

8:15pm

Backstage again. Alone, thankfully. Opening fly-by had been successful. I was also relieved to see the dressing room was empty when I returned. Much as I liked Delilah, I was in no hurry to face her right now. I decided to put our meeting behind me by opening the Extra Spicy Corn Crisps and scoffing the lot. Received a small shock when I opened my snack pack and found a drawing of the tarot's Fool on top. Underneath was a green macaron and a note from Mathilde. It said:

Happiness you cannot buy.
Macarons you can. Mx

Had no idea what Mathilde's note meant. Was it a message? A riddle? Who knows?

Ate the macaron though.

It was delicious.

8:30pm

Could I *really* burn someone? Like a dragon in a storybook?

9:00pm

Dmitri's voice boomed out over the loudspeaker: '*Brace yourselves, boys and girls. On your feet, ladies and gentlemen. This is one demon you do* NOT *want to insult! Please welcome the Master of Mayhem, the Prince of Pranks, the world's one and only flying demon . . .* ***FIRE BOY!***'

I exploded into the Big Top.

Swooping low over the crowd, a tail of orange and red flames fanned behind me, lost in my jet stream. I blazed through three loops of the circus tent, flaming circuits of air-sprints, spins, zigzags, nose-dives and somersaults.

As I soared above the stands, rows of cameras filmed my fly-over. I recognised familiar faces dotted among the crowd: Sadie cheering as I passed; Hussein, his headphones on, flashing me a thumbs up from the control booth; Mum clapping; Max Goldman and Andrew in box seats grinning with glee as I rounded the bend.

I gazed down at the crowd below me.

Was Delilah right?

Should I destroy Sloane Sixsmith?

Would I recognise a shape-shifter if I saw her

in the stalls?

And that's how it happened. As I searched the crowd for a mousey-haired woman with a forked tongue, I didn't watch where I was going.

I flew into the centre post.

The scoop lights which hung from its mid-line exploded. Bulbs burst into a shower of sparks and their casings melted. The wires connected to the scoop lights split. Ripped free from their mounts, they fizzed and snapped like snakes.

The power cut out and the Big Top went dark. Except for me, of course. I was on fire.

The lighting support, a metal cone which held the scoop lights in place, came loose. It fell, landing with a thud and a shout.

A Russian shout.

'Dmitri!' I cried, darting to the ground and extinguishing my flames. I found him on his side, his leg trapped under a lump of metal. It was twisted awkwardly, like a tree snapped in two after a storm.

My head spun. I averted my eyes, afraid that I might be sick, and threw my arms around him. 'Dmitri!' I sobbed. 'I am so so sorry.'

He opened one eye. 'Go – before she comes.

Before the newspapers and cameras arrive. It is not safe for you here.'

'I can't!' I cried. 'I can't leave you like this! I don't care about the papers.'

'I do,' Dmitri winced, his teeth clenched. Already he looked pale and white. 'For me, I am asking you. Go.'

I struggled to my feet. 'For you.'

'For me,' he said.

As I ignited, a mob of photographers circled us. Cameras popped and flashed. I ascended slowly, head down, my tears turning to flames. I drifted towards the exit and flew out into the cold November night.

I flew over the Big Top and Central Park.

I glided above the ice skating rink at the Rockefeller Center and over the Empire State Building.

I passed Greenwich Village and Wall Street.

I sailed over the bay and headed towards Liberty Island, where the Statue of Liberty stood. It seemed wrong to stand on her crown, so I settled for the torch.

It was the first time I had flown outside the Big Top in over a month and I had forgotten how different it was flying in the rain or against the wind. Mum had been the one to insist I restrict my flying to the Big Top. It would keep my identity a secret, she said. Plus, it was easier for people to believe Fire Boy was an act if my powers were contained to the tent.

But those things didn't matter to me any more.

Not after what I'd done.

And if a downpour put out my flames or a gust of wind blew me into a building, I didn't care. I deserved it.

I had hurt Dmitri, the kindest man I had ever known, because of my own carelessness. I had been so stupid.

Flames snuffed, I sat shivering in the cold wind, arms curled round my legs, staring out at the city.

Two months ago, Sadie, Hussein and I had roamed over the rooftop in our old apartment block. Nothing was going to stand in our way until we mastered our new powers. I blasted chimney bricks with fire-bolts and struggled to fly. Sadie juggled pebbles with her mental powers, twisting them into spirals and spheres. Hussein zapped rusting aerials and decaying satellite dishes with electricity, bringing them back to life. What a lark that had been, a right laugh.

And now I had abandoned Dmitri on the circus floor, his leg snapped in two – and it was all my fault.

I closed my eyes and tried to blot out the memory of what I had done.

How long I sat there with my head buried in my hands, I can't tell you. I was so lost in my own thoughts that I took no notice of the weather or the time or the three Homeland Patrol helicopters speeding towards me.

I did hear their radio speakers though.

'YOU ARE TRESPASSING ON GOVERNMENT PROPERTY. DEFACING THE STATUE OF LIBERTY IS A FEDERAL CRIME AND YOU SHALL BE PROSECUTED.'

Blinded by the glare, I blinked into their searchlights and shielded my eyes. 'Are you talking to me?' I shouted.

'NO, I'M TRYING TO GET THE ATTENTION OF THE OLD MAN IN THE CAFÉ. **YES! I'M TALKING TO YOU!**'

'I'm just asking,' I complained. 'There's no need to shout.'

'WHO ELSE IS WITH YOU?'

'I'm by myself,' I said.

'I DON'T BELIEVE YOU.'

'That's a bit harsh, isn't it? People usually wait

until they get to know me before they accuse me of lying.'

'IF YOU'RE ALONE, HOW DID YOU CLIMB ON TO THE TORCH BY YOURSELF?'

'I didn't climb. I flew here. I'm Fire Boy.'

'THE CIRCUS STAR? I DON'T BELIEVE YOU.'

'It's true,' I said.

'YEAH, RIGHT. PROVE IT THEN.'

I got to my feet. I lit one hand.

'WOAH!'

I lit the other.

'HEY! HOW DID YOU DO THAT?'

'You wouldn't believe me if I told you.' I considered apologising for trespassing – I had assumed Miss Liberty was open to visitors – but you get to a point where you've said sorry so often that it loses its meaning. So I jumped.

It was a long fall. Like, seriously long. Long enough to take a photo of yourself in mid-air and still keep falling.

Halfway down, I ignited.

I pulled out of the dive and skimmed over the water.

It was time to return to Manhattan and Central Park. I wanted to go home.

I needed to see Mum and talk to Dmitri. If this was the end of Fire Boy, the circus star, so be it. This – the flying, the freedom of soaring over a sea or city – it was needed for more than just circus tricks. It was a gift I couldn't waste.

Maybe I could learn how to be a beacon for good too.

When I returned to Central Park, the Big Top was dark and the circus grounds deserted. There were no lights on at Dmitri's either, so I landed behind our caravan. I could see Mum through the window.

She met me at the door. 'Aidan! Where have you been? It's almost midnight. I was so worried.'

'Out,' I said. 'How's Dmitri?'

Mum's eyebrows pinched together, an expression which told me I would not like what she had to say. 'He's fractured his tibia. Because of the angle he fell at, he might have ruptured ligaments in his knee. It wasn't pretty.'

Dmitri.

For forty years he shared a caravan with a bear. Did he ever need to go to A&E when he roomed with Zarathustra? No. Sure, he had a few knocks – claw scars on his forearms, a dodgy shoulder and a bit of his ear was missing – but it wasn't until he met me that he . . . that he . . .

Gathering me in her arms, Mum led me inside.

We collapsed on to the sofa. From the windowsill, Lemon watched us, her tail stiff. Wanting a cuddle, I patted the cushion next to me. She blinked and stayed put.

Cats.

When do they ever do what you want?

'Are Sadie and Hussein here?' I asked.

'They're in bed. They wanted to stay up until you got back, but I insisted. They were exhausted,' Mum said. 'Where did you go?'

I told her about the Statue of Liberty and she told me about Dmitri's leg break: the ride in the ambulance; the position of his leg when they found him; the probable severity of the break; which of her fellow paramedics attended to him; and how long he ought to expect to be in a cast. Gory details were *not* spared.

'Did Sloane Sixsmith show up?' I asked.

'Were you expecting her?' Mum answered.

I explained how Dmitri told me to fly away before Sloane arrived. 'He seemed to think she was in the Big Top. Delilah had mentioned her too.'

'Delilah?' blinked Mum. 'When did you speak with her?'

There didn't seem any point in holding back so I told Mum about the visit Delilah paid me backstage before the show.

'What was I thinking?' I moaned. 'Delilah had me so wound up that I was searching for Sloane in the stands when I flew over the crowd. That's why I collided with the lighting. I was trying to spot her instead of watching where I was going.'

I buried my head in Mum's lap.

'I let Dmitri down,' I sobbed. 'The circus too. No one will speak to me again.'

'Hush,' Mum said, cradling my head. 'Don't say that. Accidents happen. No one – least of all Dmitri – feels you let them down.'

Mum kissed the top of my head.

'Trust me. I *know* Dmitri will understand. That man will stand by you through thick and thin.'

She was far less complimentary about Delilah. In fact, I couldn't remember seeing her so livid.

'How dare that girl tell you to burn Sloane!' she raged. 'What kind of a person encourages you to maim another human being? You tell me: who's the real monster here – Delilah Jones or Sloane Sixsmith?'

Lemon hopped on to the table, her back arched and hissing.

'You're scaring Lemon,' I said.

'Am I?' Mum snorted. 'I don't know what's got into that cat. She's been acting strange all evening.'

'And Delilah's no *monster*. She's worried about me, that's all.'

Mum stiffened. She opened her mouth to reply, then checked herself.

Meanwhile, Lemon prowled across the table like she was after a mouse. Instead of pouncing on a rodent though, she began nuzzling the straps on a green knapsack hanging off the back of a chair, pawing at it as if she were trying to claw it open.

'What's in the bag?' I asked. 'Sardines?'

'I don't know,' Mum replied. 'I assumed it was yours. Sadie dropped it off after the show.'

I slid off the sofa to check.

I pulled the bag away from Lemon and looked inside. It was my kit, the clothes I'd left behind in the dressing room.

'Ai-dan,' Mum said from behind me, stressing the second syllable of my name – a sure sign that the following questions were significant, and that my replies would be picked over thoroughly. 'What did you say when Delilah told you to burn Sloane Sixsmith?'

I pulled my balled-up jeans out of the knapsack and rooted around for my phone.

'I told you already, didn't I?'

'No,' Mum said. 'You didn't.'

There were three messages on my phone.

'Aidan?' Mum prompted.

I looked up at her. 'I thought about it – burning Sloane, I mean – but I could never see myself doing it to her or anyone else.' I paused. 'Except maybe Granny.'

'You wouldn't!' Mum cried.

'Oh, yes, I would!'

'I don't believe you,' Mum said.

'It wouldn't be a *serious* burn – it's not as if I want to toss Granny on a pit and roast her alive. I'm not a *savage*.' I stopped, grinning at the most wonderful possibilities on offer. 'A good hot nip is what I have in mind, like a wasp sting – a really angry wasp's sting, two or three of them, maybe – a sting that would make her jump out of her chair and shout YOW!'

'You're awful,' Mum chuckled.

'A little burn wouldn't violate the terms of my sacred oath.'

'This is true,' Mum replied.

When I first told Mum about my powers, she asked me to make a sacred oath promising to only use my fiery powers for good.

A short note about sacred oaths:

Should you ever develop a superpower of your own – perhaps you find a magic ring that gives you the power to stop time or a blast from a radioactive fallout transforms you into the Invisible Girl or Boy – however you come about your powers, heed my advice: when your mum insists you vow to use your power only for good, walk away. Stick your earphones in and move swiftly towards the door. Learn from my mistake, friend. An oath-free life offers plenty of exciting possibilities. One day, you will thank me.

I checked my texts.

One message was from Sadie. CALL ME. Sx, it said.

'Anyway,' I said, scrolling to the next message. 'How is *burning* Sloane Sixsmith going to help? I don't buy the let's-hunt-her-down thing. Has Sloane tried to seize power or take over the world? No. Okay, the shape-shifting and memory-stealing is a little creepy, but so what? People might say the same thing about me and fire. My powers don't make me evil, do they?'

'No, they don't,' Mum said quietly.

The next text was from Hussein. Talk soon, it said with a worried emoji face stuck on.

'If you want to know the truth, I feel sorry for Sloane. First her boyfriend betrayed her, then the legendary tree which she identified is destroyed. Everyone assumes she's a villain who's after secrets and power. But why? I don't see any evidence of it.'

'Neither do I,' Mum said.

The last message was from Mum. It was longer than the others.

Darling. I'm in A&E with Dmitri. Sadie and Hussein are with me. It's busy so he probably won't be seen until after midnight. Call me if you want to talk. Dmitri sends his love and tells you not to worry. It was an accident, nothing more. He's worried about you. Mxxxx

I read it twice, feeling a prickling sensation at the back of my neck. Slowly, I turned round. 'Mum . . .'

I stopped, stunned into silence.

In Mum's place sat Sloane Sixsmith.

Show and tell

My legs buckled and I staggered backwards.

Lemon sprang out of my way as my temperature spiked. Sparks fizzed from my fingers and I scorched the floorboards where I fell. My demon costume glowed red. Smoke steamed out of my bottom – at least, I hoped it was smoke. So, yes. You could say I was a little surprised to find Sloane Sixsmith in Mum's robe and T-shirt sitting across from me.

'W–w–what have you done with my mother?' I stammered.

'Nothing,' Sloane said. 'She's at the hospital. Your mother remained with Dmitri until the stretcher came. When the paramedics wheeled him away, your mother and friends got into the ambulance after him.'

'Is that when you . . . when you and Mum . . .'

'Made contact?' offered Sloane.

'Yeah.'

'No. When we were filing out of the Big Top, I overheard the tight-rope walker ask your mother where you had gone. It was so dark and crowded that I doubt your mum knew we touched.' A hint of a smile flitted over Sloane's features. 'Fortunate us meeting like that, wouldn't you say?'

Not from where I was sitting.

My fists became two balls of flames. 'If you hurt my mother, I swear I'll—'

'I *don't* hurt people,' Sloane protested. 'I would *never* harm anyone. Please, Aidan,' she begged. 'You must believe me.'

I turned the heat on my fist-flames down to simmer. 'When you . . . *make contact*, what happens to the other person? Do their memories vanish?'

'No,' Sloane said. '*I* change, not the other person. My powers allow me to imitate – to copy-and-paste, not delete. When I inhabit another identity, I have access to a person's memories. When I revert back to myself, the connection is broken, though traces of the people I became remain.'

'Prove it,' I said, extinguishing my flames and sitting down across from Sloane. 'If you dipped into my mum's memories, you must know a few things about me.'

Sloane said, 'I know you like football, comics and a snack of cheese on toast when you come home from school. You put Tabasco sauce, not ketchup, on chips. You roll your clothes into balls instead of folding them and you still struggle with your times tables.'

'Not bad,' I replied, 'though that could be any boy my age.'

'You want more?' Sloane said. 'When you were four, you had an imaginary friend called Mr Tootles. You sucked your thumb until you were six and still like to sleep with a light on. On your ninth birthday a rumbly tummy and bad case of diarrhoea ended with—'

I held my hand up. 'You can stop there. You've made your point.'

Lemon reappeared, climbing over my legs and settling into my lap, her eyes on Sloane throughout. As I stroked her flanks, a plan began to take root.

The basic premise of this cunning stratagem:
When confronted by a superpowered opponent, a tiger-cat might prove a useful ally.

Could it actually work though?

Relying on Lemon to do my bidding was a big ask. Like most cats, Lemon tended to go her own way, ignoring my requests and shunning attempts to learn tricks. (Three years I spent trying to teach her to moonwalk! Three years! Is one dance step that much to ask?) One couldn't rule out the possibility of her swapping sides either, should Sloane happen to have a tin of sardines on her. Still, the chance to have Lemon play Robin to my Batman was too tempting to let pass.

Sloane got to her feet.

'What are you doing?' I asked.

'I need you to trust me, Aidan, if we are going to work together.'

Sloane took off Mum's robe, revealing the T-shirt and jeans she wore underneath. 'That means no secrets. I know about you and your friends, Sadie and Hussein, and what they can do . . .'

Alarm rippled through me. Sloane did know

about Sadie and Hussein!

'I know about Lemon's powers too.'

And Lemon – blast it! Goodbye tag-team!

'But you know little about me.' Sloane's shoulder-length brown hair began to shrink, reappearing as short, thick spikes, white and tinged with pale green.

'When I first woke in hospital, the doctors feared me. The nurses called me a *monstruo*, a freak.'

Her eyes widened, her mouth lengthened. Rows of round and oval scales emerged on her skin.

'No one visited me. No one spoke to me. My colleagues at Cambio abandoned me. Ash Aitkens – the man who I sacrificed everything for – betrayed me.'

Her skin colour darkened into a vivid green. Patches of shimmering blue and yellow appeared. Black stripes coiled around her arms and neck.

'This is what I am now, stripped of disguises,' Sloane declared. 'A human chameleon.'

Lemon scrambled out of my lap and scooted behind the chair.

I'll be honest. My first instinct was to join her. It was like an alien or the creature from the black lagoon had suddenly appeared in my sitting room. I held my nerve though, reflecting on what Sloane had said about being abandoned. I didn't want to be another name on her list.

I nudged forward. 'Can I touch your scales?'

Sloane held out her arm.

Her skin was as rough and leathery as snakeskin. When I placed my fingers on her forearm, its colours stirred like dye drops mixed in water. Her vivid green skin faded to a freckly white – a mirror of my own skin.

'This is amazing!' I cried. 'How do you do that?'

'I don't,' Sloane said, her skin returning to green as I stepped away from her. 'It's a reflex.'

I moved further back, trying to see how close I needed to be for Sloane's skin to change colour. 'What's the connection between you and chameleons?' I asked.

'Connection?'

'It's how the serum works, right? There's a link between your nature and the power you develop. Sadie's clever so she became a telekinetic. Hussein loves gaming, so he became a human computer and me, well, I just—'

'Light up a room?' Sloane said, finishing for me. 'That's what your mother would say.'

'Yeah,' I said. 'She would.'

Mum.

I pictured her in a crowded A&E room, Sadie and Hussein beside her, watching out for Dmitri, making sure he got the best care on offer.

Dmitri.

'I ought to go,' I said, walking towards the door. 'I should go and see how Dmitri is.'

Sloane grabbed hold of my arm. 'No! Not yet! Let me finish what I came here to say. I've risked so much to see you and I don't know how much time I have left before I . . .'

Sloane let go of my arm. She slumped to the floor clutching her head as if she were in pain.

'I don't know how much longer I can go on,' Sloane sobbed, and she began to cry.

This I was not expecting.

I sloshed milk into the mug and mixed it in with a spoon. 'Here,' I said, pushing it towards Sloane. 'Have some of this.'

I had no idea whether tea would help or not in

this situation – hot chocolate with a healthy sprinkling of marshmallows is my late-night beverage of choice – but it's what Mum would have done.

'Thank you,' Sloane sniffed.

Was it odd sitting across from a woman with green scales for skin, a lizard mouth and white spiked hair?

Not really.

Looking into Sloane's yellow eyes, I remembered the banner Miss Spatchcock hung over her smartboard. It said: **Don't be afraid of being different. Be afraid of being like everyone else.**

Fair dues to Sloane. She was seriously *different* – we're talking different in great big capital letters. But it was everyone else who was the problem.

Literally.

Shape-shifting came at a cost, Sloane explained. She could assume the shape of any person alive – speak like them, walk and talk like them, even share the same memories – but when she shifted back to herself, they never entirely went away.

'When I'm alone, it's as if there's a crowd inside my head,' Sloane confessed. 'I can't sit down to eat without setting off an argument. One says she's glucose-intolerant. One insists on fried foods. One demands peanut butter on toast each morning and another only wants grapefruit.'

'Mum tends to skip breakfast, if that's any help,' I said.

Sloane rubbed her forehead. 'It's not just breakfast, Aidan. It's *everything*. Taking on your mother was almost too much for me. I am at my limit. If I take on another identity, I'm afraid I might lose my own.'

I was fairly certain at this point that I wasn't sitting down with a supervillain who could overpower the world. I wasn't sure what to say though.

'Can I get you some aspirin?' I asked.

'No,' Sloane sniffed. 'I'll be fine.'

Lemon must have sensed the change in mood too. Up she jumped on to the table, rubbing the back of her neck against the scales on Sloane's arms.

Sloane smiled.

I should have known Lemon was the best medicine on offer. As Sloane stroked Lemon's fur, the scales on her arms turned into ginger and white hairs.

Amazing.

I said, 'are these voices inside your head telling you to destroy the last drops of serum?'

Sloane's eyes shot open. 'No! I'm not *mad*, Aidan. The memories and lives of the people I carry with me are a cross I must bear. They make *my* life difficult, no one else's.'

Sloane's scales flared and shimmered. Her yellow eyes glowed and the white spikes running down the back of her head bristled.

Frightened, Lemon scooted away.

'I am not the threat! It's presidents and prime ministers who crave power, not me. They are the ones scrambling to get hold of my serum. Powerful men like Clayton Jones who want to clone it.'

'Clayton Jones?' I gasped. 'He knows about the jar of Nature's Own?'

'Yes,' Sloane said. 'Your friend, Agent Whittaker, knew, but wasn't at liberty to say. Jones wants the serum for himself. He believes it will allow him to live forever.'

Stunned?

Reader, I was floored.

I felt like a right fool, a Grade A sucker who had been taken to the cleaners once again.

Despite that, there was only one thing I wanted to know.

'Was Delilah in on this plan too?' I asked.

But at that very moment we heard the pad of footsteps passing under our window.

Someone was outside our caravan.

Sloane vanished. One moment she was in front of me and the next – *whoosh* – she was gone. As I wondered whether Sloane had teleported to another location, feeling jealous that she might have *two* superpowers, I noticed how the wall seemed nearer. Intrigued, I looked again. This time I spotted her. Pressed against the wall, arms out flat, her skin colour was an exact match to the oak panels behind her, right down to the grooves in the hardwood.

'It's Homeland Patrol!' Sloane whispered. She glanced nervously at the door. 'They were all over the airport when I arrived! They must have followed me here!'

I checked the window. The grounds were so dark, there was no way of telling whether one person was outside, or twenty. 'Wait here,' I said. 'I'll have a look.'

Opening the door a crack, I slipped out. Lemon saw her chance and nipped out with me, eager to explore the grounds.

It was pitch-black. A thick mist had rolled in, hanging over the caravans and smothering the light of the moon and stars. Lamplight glowed in the windows of two caravans: Mathilde's and Dead-Eye's. Everyone else, it seemed, was asleep.

Lemon ambled towards the fence, prowling low to the ground. I followed, unsure whether her cat eyes had spotted someone or she was merely stalking a midnight snack. Figuring I would be able to see more from the air, I ignited and swooped after her.

Lemon headed for the 'recycling centre' – three large bins for bottles, plastic and waste that were shared by the caravan dwellers. The odds that Lemon was pursuing a rat increased greatly.

I wasn't far wrong.

A figure emerged from the shadows. He was alonc and had a black beanie pulled over his thick skull, a black windbreaker zipped up, black jeans on and black boots. Even his phone was black, a phone that he was holding out in front of him, as if he had just finished filming . . .

'GOTCHA!' he cried. 'HELLO, SWEENEY! Or should I say . . . *FIRE BOY!*'

'Mulch?' I gasped in disbelief. Descending, I extinguished my flames. 'What are you doing here?'

'Ha!' Mulch roared. 'I'm getting the scoop of the century, that's what! Wait until Spatchcock and those bozos see MY NAME on the front page of the *Daily Herald*.'

He stepped away from the bins and glared at me. 'I always knew it was you, Sweeney. Ever since that night in the Big Top. No one believed me, but I knew – and now that I have the proof right here, I'm going to tell EVERYONE! Three nights – THREE NIGHTS – I've been shivering here in the dark, waiting for you to make a mistake. I should be out on the town with my mum and dad or ringing room service in the hotel – did I tell you we're staying at The Plaza, THE best hotel in New York? – but no, I've been hiding behind these rubbish bins, waiting to nab you on fire when you weren't looking.'

A gloating Mitchell Mulch is hard to stomach. The urge to turn him into ash was so strong that I could taste the flames in my mouth.

But it died quickly.

After Dmitri's accident and coming face-to-face with Sloane Sixsmith, Mulch didn't seem that important any more.

'Go ahead, Mulch,' I said. 'Take the video to the *Herald* if it's that important to you. Maybe it's for the best my secret's out in the open.'

Lemon spat a furball at Mulch's feet which, more or less, summed up the way I felt. Lemon and I walked away.

Mulch ran after us.

'Not so fast, Sweeney,' Mulch said, tugging on my arm. 'It doesn't have to end this way. I don't have to go to the newspapers. I'm open to offers.'

'Offers?' I scowled. 'What are you talking about?'

'Tell me how you do it,' Mulch pleaded. 'Show me how to burn and I won't tell a soul that you're Fire Boy.'

Mulch on fire?

The stuck-up git would be a tyrant. People would be forced to bend to his will or face his flames.

'NOT. A. CHANCE.' I wrenched my arm free and walked away.

Mulch raced after me. 'Come on, Sweeney,' he begged. 'It can't be that hard, not if you can do it.'

I rolled my eyes.

Mulch dropped to his knees. 'Please!' he begged. 'I'll be your best friend.'

'Enjoy your reward money, Mulch,' I said. 'I always knew you were a snitch.'

Mulch's face went dark. His ratty eyes blazed. 'You're afraid, aren't you?'

'*Afraid*? Of you?'

'Yes!' Mulch scowled, hopping to his feet and shaking his fists at me. 'You know I'd make a better Fire Boy than you – that's why you won't tell me!'

I laughed. The cheek of him! Using my index finger like a fire wand I looped a ring of flames around Mulch. By the time he opened his mouth to scream, the fire was gone.

'Go home, Mulch. Go back to The Plaza. You are the last person on the planet I would ever share my fire secrets with.'

For the second time that night, I walked away.

Mulch raged and swore. He got so angry that he charged after us, only this time he didn't try to pick on me.

He chose Lemon.

Mulch pulled his leg back and aimed a kick at Lemon's backside.

Note to reader:

You see, I wasn't exaggerating when I called Mulch a low-life rotter, was I?

Cats, of course, are quick.

Mulch missed.

By now, however, Mulch was severely testing the limits of my Sacred Oath. I was sorely tempted to smite him down with fire, but reconsidered.

Lemon could fight her own battles.

As Mulch pulled his leg back for another kick, I bent down to scratch Lemon's ear and said the magic word, 'Pushkin'.

Wisely, Mulch did not follow through.

His target – a medium-sized ginger tabby – had disappeared. In her place loomed a full-grown tiger. Thrown off-balance by stopping his kick in mid-stride, Mulch slipped. He fell, landing on his bum.

The tiger stepped forwards.

Lemon let out a mighty *ROAR!* in Mulch's face,

spraying him with tiger breath and blowing his black beanie off his head.

A cringing Mulch stared up at the tiger standing over him. His face was a sickly grey and the tuft of hair above his forehead had gone white. He seemed unable to speak.

Lemon snarled. Drool dripped out of the sides of her mouth. She flashed her sharp teeth.

'Leave him, girl,' I said, patting the thick fur around Lemon's shoulders. 'You don't want to eat him. He's rotten to the core.'

I led her away. This time we didn't look back.

When I returned to the caravan, Sloane was gone. I gingerly ran a hand over the walls and called her name, but there was no answer.

I collapsed on to the sofa. Lemon (a cat again) joined me. As she padded over my legs, I sent two texts.

A text message sent from Aidan Sweeney to Mum at 00:14am:

I'm home. Thanks for looking after Dmitri. You're the best. Please tell D that I am so so sorry. Ax

A text message sent from Aidan Sweeney to Sadie Laurel-Hewitt and Hussein Aziz at 00:15am:

MUST talk. IMPORTANT. You will NOT believe who came to see me.

I draped my arm over Lemon and was asleep within seconds.

I woke to find a helmet-haired, red-faced, cigar-chomping old woman standing over me.

'Out of bed, you lazy lump! And be quick about it or I'll grind you into matchsticks!' growled Granny, booting the underside of the sofa.

I fell, landing with my head and shoulders on the floor and my feet still stuffed under a cushion. Through the porthole I could see a brilliant blue sky. Sunlight streamed in, casting a golden spotlight on Lemon (in cat form) lying on her side. As I rubbed the sleep out of my eyes, the memories of last night returned in a mad, cinematic rush, a trailer to a film I did NOT want to see. I had got as far as Sloane's visit when a poke in the ribs brought me back to the present.

'Don't lie there, boy!' scolded Granny. *Swish* went her walking stick over my head. 'Get up!

Everyone's talking about you.'

'They are?'

'Read this,' Granny cackled, tossing a *Daily Herald* at me. 'Someone at that paper doesn't like you.'

The front page had a photo of Fire Boy flying over the Big Top. Underneath a headline bellowed:

BUST UP IN BIG TOP!

FURIOUS FIRE BOY ATTACKS RINGMASTER!

Last night Fire Boy brought TERROR to Zarathustra's Travelling Circus. The flaming daredevil plunged the Big Top into darkness during a mad frenzy. Witnesses say the fiery maniac burnt through the circus tent's electric wiring on a whim! Then, under the cover of darkness, the flaming fiend broke his Russian boss's leg by hurling a circus light at him. The ringmaster was reportedly carried off on a stretcher, seriously injured.

Sources tell the *Daily Herald* that the fire-loving weirdo is demanding more money and is prone to tantrums when he doesn't get his way.

Perhaps his demands for more cash have been refused and he's turned to violence? Apparently, Fire Boy flew off in a sulk immediately afterwards, leaving other cast members to clean up his mess.

Pages 2, 3, 4, 5 and 6 were (respectively): a photo of a worried-looking crowd queuing to leave; an image of Dmitri on a stretcher with Mum and Mathilde on each side; a snap of the Krazy Klowns sweeping bits of glass and metal from the centre ring; an aerial shot of the Big Top lit up at night; and an old picture of me hovering in mid-air with firecrackers in my hands.

On page 7, there was a call to throw me in prison.

An Editorial

Fire Boy showed New Yorkers why no one should trust a pyromaniac with a jet pack. After sabotaging the circus and injuring his boss, the cowardly firebug did a runner. The *Daily Herald* says, lock up Fire Boy now before he burns our great city to the ground!

A nasty smirk skidded across Granny's cruel lips as she watched me reading. 'Your circus days are numbered, boy. No one will want you around after last night.'

She was wrong.

The very next moment, Sadie and Hussein rushed in. I threw my arms around them. The three of us stayed locked together like that for a long time.

'You shouldn't believe everything you read, Granny,' I said. 'Nothing in this article is true.'

'Ho, ho, ho!' Granny laughed. 'What does that matter? The truth has nothing to do it with it, boy. It's about winners and losers, us and them. It's all about picking sides and, right now, no one wants you on their team.'

Granny grunted, made a rude noise and stomped off to her room.

'Tell me about Dmitri,' I said.

Hussein and Sadie quickly filled me in.

When the ambulance had carried Dmitri away, the entire circus followed. They spent the night in A&E with him, waiting to hear about his leg.

That news sent a tremor through me. My tummy

knotted and I felt the colour drain from my face. I was almost too afraid to ask if he would be able to walk again.

Sadie rushed to reassure me. 'Dmitri's fine. Don't worry. They reset the bone and repaired his knee. The doctors said Dmitri was a tough old bear and would be on his feet in no time. Your mother said not to go anywhere, that Dmitri ought to be discharged soon and he's looking forward to seeing you.'

Dmitri back at Zarathustra's!

I practically danced with joy! I felt flames rekindling inside me, a warm ruddy glow that left me feeling like a new person. What a load off my mind that was!

'What about you, mate?' Hussein asked. 'Where did you go? Everyone was wondering.'

We swapped roles. This time I told the story and the two of them listened. I left nothing out – my afternoon at Frontier Towers (until now I had only skimmed over those details. Sadie and Hussein were not the biggest fans of Delilah, so the less I said the better); meeting Delilah backstage ('I told you not to trust her,' Sadie snapped); landing on top of the Statue of Liberty ('Epic!'); discovering

Mum was Sloane Sixsmith in disguise ('Oh. My. God.'); and then, to top it off, finding Mulch hiding behind the bins.

'That's mad,' Sadie muttered.

'Mate, what is it about you? Trouble just seems to find you,' Hussein said.

Tell me about it.

I left Sloane's revelations – her struggles with her powers and her inside information on Clayton Jones – for last.

Sadie took an interest in Sloane, asking me what she looked like, how she changed shape and who the other people locked inside her head were. 'What must that be like,' Sadie wondered, 'having someone else's identity bubble up inside you and speak?'

Hussein focused more on Clayton Jones and the threat of him cloning the serum. 'It's possible,' he mused, 'though I am surprised he expects to be given the power of regeneration or eternal youth. Our abilities suit our personalities, but it's not as if we get to choose them.'

'I guess rich guys are used to getting their way,' I said.

'And their granddaughters,' said Sadie, her eyebrow arching like a long curling question mark. 'It looks to me as though *they* get whatever they want too. Haven't you noticed that while you've been busy with Delilah, you've completely forgotten about us?'

Huh? This was news to me.

I am tempted not to write down what Sadie told me next. It still pains me to recall it and to realise how I had failed my two best mates. You see, veering into the lighting on that climactic night in the Big Top wasn't the only wrong turn I made in New York. Yes, I know it would be easier to pretend it never happened and to never mention it, but I will put it down here in black and white so that you, reader, can learn from my mistakes and be a better friend.

Distracted by the bright lights of Broadway and the perfect smile of Delilah Jones, I walked past Sadie and Hussein unaware of *their* troubles. For weeks, Sadie fumed and fretted waiting for her mother to visit her. Work, it seemed, kept getting in the way – scenes that needed to be reshot, publicity events that could not be missed. Every night Sadie cried herself to sleep.

Did I notice?

Not a bit.

Was I also aware that in the bunk below me, as I parried texts back and forth with Delilah each night, Hussein tossed and turned? Had I noticed the bags under his eyes? Was I aware that he was so homesick that he struggled to eat or sleep?

No.

I am not ashamed to admit that I wept bitter tears when Sadie told me this or that I begged their forgiveness.

They gave it, of course, because that's what friends do. At the end of the day, Sadie and Hussein are the real superheroes in this story.

Me?

I'm just a kid who can fly and burn.

Law and order

I was sitting on the loo when I learnt that the USA had banned the use of superpowers. Luckily, I had my phone with me.

Mum, Dmitri and the rest of the circus still

hadn't returned when Agent Whittaker pinged an email to everyone.

To: dmitritheringmaster@gmail.com; esweeney85@londonambulance.co.uk; sadiespeaks@gmail.com; jedimasterhussein@gmail.co.uk; hotstuff08@gmail.com

From: Agent W

Subject: WARNING!

Aidan & Co.,

Police forces and army personnel throughout the US received the following notice from Homeland Patrol this evening:

> *From today, any person displaying extra-human abilities is to be considered a threat to the safety of American citizens. Officers are allowed to use whatever force they deem necessary when apprehending such individuals.*
>
> *Examples of extra-human abilities include*

the power to fly, ignite, change shape at will, etc. Such skills are commonly referred to as 'superpowers' by the general public.

Your employer, Clayton Jones and his Frontier News group, lobbied Homeland Patrol hard for this new law. We are unsure why. I assume Sloane Sixsmith's arrival has caused a flutter. **Be on your guard.** Until you hear from me again, no more Fire Boy. In fact, none of you should use your powers from now on - under any circumstances. Homeland Patrol are a gung-ho, no-nonsense outfit and will be looking to make arrests. If they charge you with a crime, I will be unable to help you.

Stay safe,
Agent Russell R Whittaker

'No superpowers?' I bawled, as soon as I was out of the toilet. 'That's not fair!'

'It's a ruse,' Sadie hissed. 'This law isn't aimed at

Americans, it's targeting you and Sloane.'

'That's not fair either!' I cried.

'That's not the worst part,' Hussein moaned.

'There's more?' I cried. 'What could be worse than banning superpowers?'

Hussein scrolled down to an item marked *Breaking News* on his phone. 'It says there will be a live press conference from the grounds of Zarathustra's Travelling Circus shortly.'

'A press conference?' I queried. 'On what?'

Hussein checked his phone. 'It doesn't say.'

I stared out the window. The private security guards had opened the main gates and were placing a temporary fence in the centre of the caravan park. A crowd was already forming around it.

'I don't like this,' I moaned.

'Do you think Dmitri scheduled a news conference to coincide with him arriving home from hospital?' Hussein asked.

'Unlikely,' I replied. 'Dmitri is not the sort to draw attention to himself.'

Soon two television trucks and a *Frontier News* van pulled up. As their reporters and camera operators unloaded their equipment, Granny stormed out of her bedroom. 'What's going on?' she shouted. 'Who are all these people? What sort of mischief have you done now, boy?'

I ignored her and stepped outside with Sadie and Hussein for a better look.

A scrum of reporters had bunched together near a podium erected in the centre of the caravan park. Microphones and television lights surrounded it. Photographers jockeyed for space around the horde while onlookers lined the fences for a better view.

A gold Rolls Royce motored into the grounds and Frontier Security cleared a path for it. The Rolls circled the caravan park, coming to a stop opposite the podium.

Its chauffeur opened one of the back doors and out stepped Delilah Jones.

Or at least, I assumed it was Delilah.

The skateboard was gone, the jeans, sweatbands and hoodie too. In their place was a white dress, a hint of make-up and a gold locket round her neck. Her copper-red hair was as neat as a pin and she was wearing proper shoes (not trainers).

The television lights flicked on.

Delilah pulled a sheet of paper out of a pocket

and moved towards the podium.

'Ladies and gentlemen,' she began, 'I would like to read a prepared statement on behalf of my granddaddy and me.

'This morning, we discovered that Zarathustra's Travelling Circus, a theatre company which Frontier News and Media sponsors, has been accused of being in violation of a Homeland Security edict banning the use of superpowers. Specifically, the circus's flying act, Fire Boy, has been identified as a potentially superpower-fuelled performance.'

The crowd of onlookers gasped. Some shouted. One man near the front fainted.

'Superpowers?'

'Are you saying Fire Boy is *real*?'

An old man shouted, 'I don't believe it! Superpowers? Bah! This is just a publicity stunt!'

Hussein whistled. 'Bad news, mate. Looks like the girlfriend is turning you in. Tough one.'

'I knew she was false from the first moment she opened her mouth,' Sadie scoffed.

I said nothing. If I did, they would only laugh. You see, I still believed Delilah was a good person. Under all the hard-nosed, kill-or-be-killed determination beat a kind heart. And the truth is that I liked her.

A lot.

The only problem was that I didn't know *this* Delilah – the one in the dress speaking into the TV cameras.

'Delilah! Wait!' Max Goldman shouted, as he struggled to push through the crowd of spectators with Andrew hot on his heels. 'Talk to me! We can sort this out!'

A burly security guard stopped him at the blockade. 'Quiet, you!' he snarled. 'Miss Jones is talking.'

Delilah Jones cleared her throat. 'As I was saying, in order to show that Frontier News and Media – like all good Americans – stands firmly on the side of law and order, my granddaddy and I are throwing open the doors of these here caravans to Homeland Patrol's officers for investigation.'

Right on cue, three black Homeland Patrol vans pulled up behind Delilah. Out marched officers in full body armour. Each officer wore battle helmets and carried an automatic rifle. They stormed forwards, kicking down the doors of our caravans – a bit senseless, really, since the security guards had the keys to all of them – and started rampaging through our belongings.

'Can anyone tell me what Homeland Patrol are looking for?' Hussein asked.

Sadie said, 'From the way they're dressed, I'm assuming they are expecting to meet a small, hostile army.'

As luck would have it, they encountered one when two Homeland officers knocked down the door to our caravan and found Granny waiting for them, her walking stick raised and ready to fire.

'Good luck to them if they try and take Granny's widescreen TV away,' I said. 'There could be casualties.'

As reinforcements raced to assist the Homeland officers trapped inside our caravan with Granny, Delilah tried to regain everyone's attention with an announcement of her own.

'Early this morning, a source came forward with information pertaining to Fire Boy and his secret identity,' Delilah said, smiling coyly into the cameras. 'My granddaddy and I immediately contacted Homeland Patrol and asked them to locate the source of Fire Boy's superpowers.'

The sweets!

So that's what Delilah was after!

But why call in Homeland Patrol? I would have given her one if she'd just waited.

This nightmare, however, had one more sordid twist left.

The door of a black jeep belonging to Homeland Patrol opened. A smirking, big-eared ferret-face I knew all too well stepped out, blinking as his eyes adjusted to the glare of the television lights.

Mulch.

Bloody hell.

What an afternoon this was turning out to be.

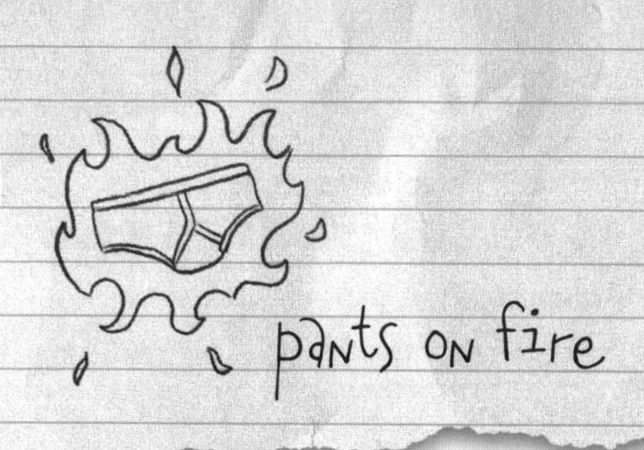

Mulch didn't waste any time. As soon as he saw me in the crowd, he turned me in.

'There he is!' Mulch thundered, pointing his finger at me. 'It's Fire Boy! Aidan Sweeney is Fire Boy! I have proof! I filmed him flying!'

A cameraman in the front row said, 'Who is that kid pointing at?'

'Me,' I sighed.

Cameras immediately swung to face me. A swarm of microphones appeared around me.

'No!' Max Goldman shouted. 'Delilah, stop! You can't let this happen!'

Everyone – bystanders, security guards, Homeland officers, reporters and photographers – all turned to stare at me.

'We can take this lot,' Sadie whispered.

Hussein nodded. 'Just say the word, mate. If we

go down, let's go down together.'

'No. Not today,' I said, walking forwards. 'This one is on me.'

A reporter stopped me. 'Hello!' she chirruped into the camera. 'This is Wanda O'Neill reporting LIVE for *Frontier News* from Central Park in the shadow of the Zarathustra's Travelling Circus's Big Top where—'

I didn't hear the rest.

Two security guards grabbed me by the arm and frogmarched me towards Delilah Jones and Mitchell Mulch.

I tried to catch Delilah's eye, but she ignored me. She kept her head pointed forwards, her gaze fixed on the horizon.

Mulch, meanwhile, was bobbing around like an organ grinder's monkey who had just found a packet of peanuts. Clearly, getting on the front page of *The Caversham Chronicle* meant a lot to him.

Delilah lowered her notes. Blinking into the lights of the television cameras she asked, 'Before we begin the unveiling, is there anything you have to say for yourself, Aidan?'

There was a *lot* I wanted to say, but when I saw how cold and remote her blue eyes were, well . . . it wasn't easy. In the end, the most I could muster was, 'So this is it, Delilah? Was this the plan from the start?'

Delilah moved away from the microphones. 'You should have given me one of those sweets the first time I asked, Aidan Sweeney,' she hissed. 'You *know* how much I wanted a superpower.'

'But Delilah—'

'No *buts*,' she snapped. 'You had your chance.'

'I thought you and I . . . I thought . . . I thought we were friends.'

The smile Delilah flashed me this time was as far from perfect as perfect gets. 'You thought wrong.'

A confused Mulch turned from Delilah to me. 'Do you two know each other?'

'Shut up,' I snarled.

'I most certainly will not,' Mulch trumpeted. He pushed past me and Delilah to face the cameras head-on. 'It's time the world knew the truth about Fire Boy!'

Strange as it may seem, having Mulch there

at that very moment was just what I needed. My encounter with Delilah had cut me to the quick. I was bruised, battered and heartbroken. Left to my own devices, I may well have thrown myself on the ground and stayed there for the rest of the afternoon. That's why having Mulch, my smirking, poop-for-brains arch-enemy was just the tonic I needed. One sneer from that idiot and I was back on my feet and ready for more.

It was time to go on the offensive.

'Before this unveiling goes any further, there's something I want to say.'

'There is?' Mulch cried.

'For a long time, it has bothered me, but now, seeing as there are so many cameras gathered around us, it seems a good time to get it off my chest.'

I took a deep, theatrical breath.

'Friends, New Yorkers and people of the world – and that includes Vialli, Fink, Jackson and the gang back in Miss Spatchcock's classroom – you deserve to know the truth.' I paused and pointed at Mulch. 'His breath stinks.'

'What?' Mulch screamed.

'It smells like he gargles with gone-off eggs and green mayonnaise.'

'How dare you!' Mulch thundered, stamping his foot.

I went on. 'Or like something died in his mouth.'

'LIAR! LIAR!'

'Floss. Buy some mints. Get yourself some mouthwash. Do something, Mulch. Ask your mum for help. She's a dentist, isn't she?'

Delilah nudged me aside. 'Thank you, Aidan, for those very colourful observations. However, we are gathered here today to hear what *Michael* has to say.'

'Yeah, *Mike*,' I said. 'We're waiting.'

Mulch's face went tomato-red. 'My name is *Mitchell*,' he snapped, slouching towards me in a furious temper.

'Hi, Mike,' I said. 'Long time no see.'

'Nothing you can say will spoil this moment for me, Sweeney,' Mulch growled.

'Whatever you say, Mike.'

Mulch grinned into the television cameras. 'Aidan Sweeney, who is a big fat LIAR, is FIRE BOY,' he declared, and only I – MITCHELL Mulch

– can prove it.' He withdrew a box of matches from his pocket and held it up. 'I shall now set fire to his clothes.'

There were a few shouts from the crowd of onlookers.

'You can't set a schoolboy on fire!'

'This is madness! Stop them!'

'Please! Someone help that poor boy!'

The Homeland officers ignored their cries and brandished their rifles. The two sneering security guards tightened their grips on my arms.

Mulch smirked, pleased that everyone's eyes were finally on him.

'Mulch,' I warned. 'There's no need for this. People *like* Fire Boy. You aren't going to win any admirers turning me in.'

'Lies and more lies!' Mulch laughed. 'That's all anyone ever gets from you, Sweeney.'

He lit a match.

'I shall now set Aidan Sweeney on fire for all the world to see. Watch how no harm comes to him, how his trousers and pants may burn, but he does not – PROVING THAT AIDAN SWEENEY IS FIRE BOY!'

Mulch lowered the match to my trousers.

Baring his teeth, he sneered at me. 'Let's see you get out of this one, Sweeney.'

Mulch was serious about lighting my pants first, the dirtbag. I had, however, made up my mind not to retaliate no matter what he or Delilah or the security guards or Homeland Patrol did to me. I felt as if I had it coming in a way. It was Dmitri who would be hobbling about for the next few months, not me. Plus there was Sadie, Hussein and Lemon to think of. The last thing I wanted was to drag them into this too.

So until then, Mulch could gloat.

I would refuse to give him the satisfaction of getting down on my knees and begging for mercy.

I stood tall and faced the cameras, which isn't easy when you have a small bush fire raging in your trousers and spreading up your legs.

And then . . .

KABOOM!

Fire burst in the sky around us.

CRASH!

A Homeland jeep exploded and rolled on to its side.

CRACK!

A bolt of fire struck the fences holding back the crowd.

Mulch gaped into the sky. 'NO! IT CAN'T BE!'

The security guards holding me ran off as fire split the earth around us. Hands free, I put out the blaze in my trousers. Were it not for my indestructible Protecto Pants, the watching TV audience would be seeing far more of Aidan Sweeney than they – or I – had bargained on.

The fire out, I raised my eyes to the sky to see what the fuss was about.

I found . . . me.

Fire Boy.

Fire Boy soared through the air, flames fanning out behind him. Like an orange and red angel, he blazed and swooped and curled.

How cool was that!

Imagine looking into a mirror one day and seeing your reflection wink at you. That's how I felt as Fire Boy dazzled and sizzled above me.

Of course, I knew it wasn't *me*.

It was Sloane.

In spite of the danger to herself, Sloane was inhabiting 'me' and my powers.

And what a show she put on!

I whistled at her loop-de-loops. I saluted her hairpin turns. I applauded her fireballs and flame-bolts!

This Fire Boy hadn't made any special oaths to her mother either.

Three fire-spritzers thrown into a Homeland officer's body armour had him shaking his hips faster than a belly dancer after three espressos and a Red Bull chaser.

Delilah stared angrily up at the sky. 'How many of those damn sweets did you give away?' she shrieked. For a second, I thought she was going to belt me, but a fizzing fire-wheel sent her racing towards the Rolls Royce.

A second one sizzled through the back of Mulch's trousers, baring his bum for all the world to see. Oh, how he screamed! It was music to my ears.

Grinning onlookers pointed their phones at Fire Boy as he shot fire-rockets into the sky and spiralled left and right. This was no trick of the light or mirrors. This was *real* flying.

Of course, the Homeland officers were real too. So were their rifles.

As they took aim, I readied myself to join the battle. A few fiery explosions at ground level ought to provide a distraction and two Fire Boys blazing away in the sky would be that much harder to hit.

I needn't have worried.

To fire a rifle, you must first undo its safety catch – and that was not going to happen with Sadie around. Every rifle and pistol jammed at the same time, giving Fire Boy the time she needed to rocket safely away.

You see, one of the major pluses of possessing telekinetic powers is that nobody can ever be certain whose mind is doing the lifting.

It was a victory, but one that came at a high cost.

The whole world now knew that Fire Boy could *really* burn and fly. It wasn't an act. It wasn't special effects. It wasn't done with mirrors.

Superpowers were *real* and *Frontier News* had broadcast it live on TV.

I never saw the Homeland officers jog out of Mathilde's gothic caravan holding a jar of sweets.

I didn't hear him shout, 'I found it, Miss Jones! I found it!'

I didn't notice him place the jar into a secure unit and whisk it into the back of his van.

Hussein filled me in on those details.

I did see Delilah drive away in the Rolls Royce though. The moment I saw the glee in her eyes, I knew Delilah had found what she came for.

The Homeland officers, the reporters, the TV trucks and the onlookers had all left. Max Goldman and Andrew scooted off after Delilah, promising to talk to her and return soon with good news if they could – Goldman still hoped to keep the circus open.

So it was just the five of us – me, Sadie with

Lemon in her arms, Hussein and Granny (who was missing a tooth, but in remarkably good form. She always did enjoy a good fight) – there to greet the rest of the circus when they returned from the hospital.

I was wondering how we were going to explain what had happened and why everyone's caravans had been turned upside-down when I saw Atlas carrying a grey-haired bear of a man in an armchair.

Dmitri!

I forgot about Delilah, Homeland Patrol, Clayton Jones and the sweets and ran to him.

Atlas placed the armchair with Dmitri on the ground. His cast, a long white plaster that ran from his foot to his thigh, stuck out straight.

I hurled myself at him. 'Dmitri,' I sobbed. 'I'm so sorry.'

'Shhh,' he said. 'I am fine. Please. No tears for me. In circus, mistakes happen. To make great show, you take risks.'

'But I wasn't watching where I was going and . . .' I choked back a sob.

'Come. We live. We learn. Steel must be beaten and hammered before it is cast in the fire, eh? You and I will become stronger because of this.' Dmitri patted my head. 'You are so warm!' he laughed. 'Like hot water bottle with hair.'

Mum pulled me away and into a hug of her own.

'I have so much to tell you,' I said.

Sadie, Hussein, Lemon and yes, even Granny, joined me. We started to fill them in on our showdown in Central Park, but the others stopped us.

Shane Kerrigan said, 'We watched it all in the hospital waiting room. Every eye was on you.'

Gareth the magician said, 'That's a fine trick you have of splitting yourself in two. You'll have to show me that one.'

Dmitri thumped his armchair. 'For now, let us put our houses in order. Tonight we meet to talk about where Zarathustra's goes next.'

Next?

I was still struggling to take it all in.

I hadn't forgotten about the sweets though – and what might happen once Clayton Jones got his hands on them. After all the risks Sloane had taken for me, the least I could do was find a way to get them back.

I needn't have worried.

True, I make more mistakes than most, but I had known what I was doing when I made Mathilde my secret-keeper.

'Do not fret. Zee jar zee girl took is fake,' Mathilde said. She patted the lining of her leather jacket. 'Zee sweets are here with me.'

I was so relieved I hugged her – a big risk when it comes to Mathilde.

'I wish I could be zere to see sem open zat jar,' she laughed.

'What did you put in it?' I asked.

'A little surprise,' Mathilde smirked.

We spent hours putting the caravans back in order. They were in a right state after Homeland Security's invasion. Drawers chucked on floors. Clothes spilt. Mattresses upended. Dmitri said none of this was new. 'A traveller's life is never easy. In some countries, we must do repairs once, twice a week.'

It made me mad hearing that. I promised Dmitri that I would make sure it never happened to Zarathustra's again.

Dmitri said, 'For many years, my bear helped. No one picks fight with bear by choice.' He patted my head and smiled. 'You are our new bear cub, eh?'

I threw my head back and roared flames. 'Not bear. Dragon,' I said.

At 6pm the circus received a notice telling us that our permit had been cancelled. We had violated the terms of our contract by harbouring a suspected superhero. Frontier News and Media gave us three days to vacate the premises.

There would be no more performances in Central Park.

Not with Clayton Jones paying the bills, anyway.

Max Goldman was beside himself. He was there in the Big Top with us too, lying down on the stage with a handkerchief across his forehead. Clayton Jones had given him a choice: stick with Frontier News and Media or remain with the circus. Max astonished us all – and himself – by choosing to stick with Zarathustra's.

'What was I thinking?' he said. 'I'm too old to grow a conscience.'

Andrew sat beside him, glowing with pride. 'I always believed in you, sir.'

Rather than eat alone in our caravans, everyone brought a meal into the Big Top and shared. What a feast! There was Jamaican jerk chicken, barbecued ribs, Moroccan couscous, heaps of greens and salad, dumplings, some HOT spicy bean chilli sauce (Thank you, Mama Yang!), individually portioned protein snacks, Welsh cakes, brownies and enough spuds to feed an army.

Lemon weaved round us, sniffing our plates. Rodrigo got out his guitar. Kenise and Mum sang and the Kerrigans told jokes. It was very merry, but throughout it all I found myself checking the entrance.

Sadie noticed. 'You're expecting Sloane to show up, aren't you?'

'Yes,' I sighed. 'I can't help wondering where she is.'

'I bet she went somewhere hot,' said Hussein. Chameleons like deserts, don't they?'

Deserts sounded remote to me. Sloane Sixsmith might possess the powers of a chameleon, but she was still human and people need each other.

Especially now.

Tomorrow, people would be waking up in a world where boys can fly. A clip of Sloane as Fire Boy descending from the sky had ricocheted round the planet. Questions about who Fire Boy was and what he could do – *An Exposé on the World's First Superhero* went one headline – were in every paper.

Little mention was made of the part Clayton Jones and Delilah played in the circus or the outing of Fire Boy.

Rich people play by different rules, I guess.

Aidan Sweeney? Yes, I got a few mentions, but it was mostly memes of me trying to put out the flames coming out of my pants. They made Hussein and Sadie laugh. Maria Vialli emailed asking if she could stick a still photo from one on the front page of the school newspaper.

Why not?

When we finished eating, Dmitri gave one of his trademark whistles and the chatter hushed. 'There is something I want to say.' Using a cane, he limped towards his ringmaster's stand in the middle of the centre ring.

'My friends, you know Zarathustra's is my life. You people here are my family. Every day I wake and say thank you world for bringing such wonderful men and women and children into my life.'

Leaning forwards on his cane, the smile lines that crinkled his face faded. His eyes flashed. 'What happened today was wrong. Soldiers – not police – broke into our homes.'

Dmitri banged his cane. 'Our Big Top is gone and soon our caravans too. Life will be hard, but we will stay in New York and survive. Because of Zarathustra's new friends – Max Goldman and his assistant, Andrew – we shall not have to leave the city. Zarathustra's will go back to its roots and be street circus, performing for free and then disappearing.'

Goldman groaned.

Andrew stood and waved. 'Thank you! I am SO happy to be here with you tonight.'

He sat down.

Dmitri tapped his cast with his cane. 'However, this brings me to my other announcement. A ringmaster must hop and skip and jump. I cannot for many months. Because of this, we have new ringmaster.'

'No!' we cried.

Dmitri waved away our shouts. 'I will return when leg healed. Until then, you need ringmaster who is young and nimble. For this, I choose Mathilde.'

Where Mathilde had been hiding, I don't know, but in she walked, wearing an all-black, iron-studded ringmaster's suit. It came with a leather mini skirt, Dr. Martens and a black bowler hat.

Climbing the steps up to the ringmaster's stand, she stood above Dmitri who threw her his cane.

Mathilde twirled and bowed. I stood and applauded and soon the others followed suit.

'Thank you,' Mathilde said. 'As I am sure you know, I always saw zis day coming.'

We laughed.

Shane said, 'Is that one of your spare suits she's wearing, Dmitri?'

Donal said, 'Yeah, Dmitri. I don't remember seeing you go round in that number.'

'Just as well,' Finbar added. 'The only mini I want to see Dmitri in has four wheels and a gear shift.'

Granny rose. 'I don't know why you're laughing!' she thundered. 'I'm not taking orders from some stroppy teenager! Go back to your crystal ball, girlie, and come back when you're older!'

The Big Top fell silent.

We waited for Dmitri to make peace – he had a way of charming Granny into doing what he wanted – but he didn't speak.

Mathilde did.

'Old woman, you have a choice. Either sit down and shut your mouth and we carry on or I shall take zat walking stick off you, chop it up, sauté it in a pan and zen feed it to you bit by bit until you swallow it whole.'

Granny sat down and shut her mouth.

I leaned in and whispered in Sadie's ear: 'I could get used to this.'

Mathilde said, 'Great times are ahead. Trust me, I know. But it will come at a price. Are you ready to fight, my friends?'

'WE ARE!' the circus shouted while Atlas ripped his T-shirt in two.

'You had better be,' Mathilde urged, her voice rising. 'An army of the night will rise and we shall defeat them, but only if we stick together.' Raising her cane, Mathilde pointed it at Lemon. As if by command, she leapt on to the ringmaster's stage, transforming into a tiger in mid-air.

Hussein leaned in and whispered in my ear: 'How did she do that?

Lemon the tiger circled round Mathilde and now she too roared.

Mathilde raised a fist in the air. 'If *Frontier News* wants a war, I say we give them one!'

Lemon roared again.

Soon all of us were on our feet and roaring with her.

'This isn't zee end,' Mathilde declared. 'It is zee beginning.'

Later that same evening

I tiptoed out the back door of the caravan. When I hit the ground, I ignited.

I rocketed into the night sky, arcing high over Central Park. I headed south.

Was I worried that Homeland Patrol might blow me out of the sky or that an army helicopter could lock on my heat trail and track me down?

No.

I felt strong – superhero strong – and I wasn't going to let anyone stand in my way.

Plus, I had promised Mum I wouldn't be long.

You see, I couldn't let it end this way. I had to see her again. Besides, Frontier Towers wasn't far and I knew she would be waiting for me.

Rule #53 from *The BIG BOOK of Superheroes*:
Superheroes never shirk their duty. They stick to their task until the very end.

I landed on the observation booth, a circular structure with tall windows, that stood on top of the main building's roof. As soon as I landed, she came out of the shadows.

'I wasn't sure if you'd come,' Sloane said, walking towards me.

I almost laughed.

'*Not* come? Where would I be if it weren't for you?'

'Really?'

'Really.'

The two of us simmered on the top deck like two red-hot torches. It was like looking into a mirror that followed you everywhere you went.

Strange.

I said, 'The serum is safe, by the way. Clayton Jones hasn't got it.'

'Good,' Sloane said. 'I wasn't looking forward to wrestling it away from Delilah.'

'Me neither.' Even with the two of us – two of me – I didn't think we could have taken on Delilah. No matter what she'd done, Delilah and I had been friends, good friends. This afternoon felt like it had been her grandfather talking, not the girl I knew. I couldn't have harmed Delilah and doubted whether Sloane could either – not while she was inside my body at any rate.

'How are the voices?' I asked.

Sloane shrugged. 'It's not too bad being you. With most people, there's a lot of clutter inside their heads. Yours is pretty empty. Outside of thoughts about food, football and fire, there's not much here.'

'I take that as a compliment,' I said. 'Clarity of mind is a rare gift. Does this mean you're going to carry on as me?'

Sloane said, 'I don't have a choice. I tried going back, but the voices inside my head were too loud. It looks like I'm you from now on.'

'Are you serious?'

'I am,' Sloane said.

'*Forever?*'

'Who knows?' Sloane shrugged.

It took a minute or two for that to sink in. When I came out of my trance, I found Sloane staring back at me.

'It looks like I have a twin brother.'

Sloane's face broke into a wide grin.

'I wonder what Mum will say!' we both shouted at the same time.

Oh, how we laughed at that!

But Sloane was much MUCH more than a twin! Sloane was Aidan Sweeney with a PhD! Aidan Sweeney with a driving licence! 'Think of the tricks you and I can play!' I cried. 'New York and London won't know what hit them!'

'Sweeney and Sweeney,' Sloane laughed, rising into the air. 'Together at last!'

'Double the fun and double the trouble!' I chimed in.

Hovering in mid-air, a sudden frown crossed Sloane's face. 'Are you sure Mum won't mind?' she asked.

'*Mind?* Are you kidding? She'll be over the moon! She loves us!'

I joined Sloane in mid-air and like two fiery stars we rocketed into the New York sky.

WAIT!

DON'T CLOSE THE BOOK JUST YET!

THERE'S MORE!

TURN THE PAGE AND SEE...

Inside Frontier towers, in her grandfather's gold bathroom, Delilah Jones gazes forlornly at her reflection in the mirror.

Her eyes are red.

Her nose is swollen. A river of snot – more snot than she dreamed could ever exist inside one person – pours from her nostrils.

Her long, luscious copper hair is now a vivid neon-green.

She sighs.

Her day had started so well. How did it end like this?

Delilah's press conference had gone down a treat. Even granddaddy had been impressed. 'There's a future for you on the board of directors at Frontier News and Media,' he'd told her afterwards.

Outing Aidan on live TV had not been easy, but she'd held her nerve. And besides, he had it coming. Aidan *knew* how badly she wanted a superpower. Yet did he once lift a finger to help her?

No, sir.

Well, Delilah Jones is not the type of girl who waits for handouts. If she sees something she wants, she takes it.

Yes, the *other* Fire Boy had been a shock – one of those friends of his, she assumed, that snarky girl or the nervous kid with the glasses – but did this second fiery avenger deter Delilah?

Not a bit.

While everyone else ran away, she had stood her ground.

It was Delilah who'd instructed the Homeland officers to find the jar Aidan had hidden and bring it to Frontier Towers.

Now *that* – the waiting – had been hard.

Knowing she was so close to becoming to possessing a superpower – to becoming the superhero she was to be – was unbearable! Why, she nearly ripped that jar out of the officers' hands and swallowed a sweet there and then.

But she didn't.

She had promised Granddaddy that he could open the jar. He was waiting for her too, so desperate to get his hands on Aidan's jar that he'd met them at the elevator in his pyjamas and slippers.

Did he say hello to Delilah?

Did he thank his granddaughter for risking life and limb to bring the jar to him?

No, sir.

He took the box and tottered off, leaving her to see off the Homeland officers. By the time she caught up with him, Clayton Jones had already opened the jar.

But there weren't four sweets inside it like Aidan had said.

There was one.

'WHERE ARE THE OTHERS?' roared Clayton Jones. 'EACH OF THOSE SWEETS ARE WORTH BILLIONS!' he screamed.

And that's when the truth all came out. Her Granddaddy had known about Cambio Laboratories, Sloane Sixsmith, the sweets and Aidan from *the very start*.

'Such a precious gift *wasted* on that fool boy! He

had no idea of the power in his hands!'

Unlike Aidan, her granddaddy was convinced that he could use the serum to choose a power.

'Only the weak accept the fate they're handed. The strong-minded choose their destiny,' Clayton Jones declared. 'When I bite into this sweet, I shall decide what power I shall have . . . and I choose youth. Regeneration! That's what I want! I shall be the man who lives forever!'

He squeezed his pudgy fingers into the jar.

'We shall hunt down the other three tomorrow,' he promised. Her grandfather planned on handing the rest over to a team of genetic scientists at Frontier Medical. 'Once we learn how to clone this serum, I shall become the richest man ever to walk this earth.'

Clayton Jones plucked out the single sweet. 'Goodbye, old age. Hello, youth.'

He opened his mouth.

Delilah always had been quick.

She moved like lightning and snatched it out of her granddaddy's hand.

Presidents, prime ministers, senators, politicians and businessmen and women might cower in the presence of the chairman of Frontier News and Media, Clayton Jones.

Not Delilah.

She swallowed it in one go.

That was an hour ago, an hour filled with threats, streams of snot, green hair and . . . no superpowers.

Delilah takes a deep breath.

Wiping her nose once more, she opens the bathroom door.

A frothing, red-faced, purple-veined Clayton Jones waits. 'HOW DARE YOU . . .' The old man stops. He gapes at his granddaughter. 'Good lord, Delilah. What have you done to your hair?'

'They tricked us,' Delilah sniffs. 'There was no serum inside the sweet.'

Her granddaddy's eyes bulge. Spittle dribbles from his lips. He takes a deep breath and then explodes. 'THEY TRICKED *US*?' he thunders. 'DO THEY KNOW WHO I AM? I SWEAR I WILL GRIND THAT BOY AND HIS CIRCUS INTO DUST!'

Delilah blows her nose furiously into a tissue.

'Aidan didn't do this,' she says. 'He can't think

that far ahead. It was one of the others.'

'Was it that Sixsmith woman?' Clayton Jones asks, watching his granddaughter trumpet another volley of snot into her napkin.

'I don't know.'

On the far wall, a wide-screen television broadcasts a *Frontier News* bulletin – *America in Crisis*. As the newscaster speaks, a video of Fire Boy flying over Central Park plays behind her.

Pushing past her grandfather, Delilah crosses to the windows overlooking Central Park. Two fiery stars shoot past before her eyes.

'But I promise you this,' she declares. 'Aidan Sweeney and his friends are going to rue the day they dared to cross Delilah Jones.'

WILL DELILAH JONES FINALLY ACQUIRE A SUPERPOWER AND WREAK REVENGE ON AIDAN?

MIGHT SLOANE SIXSMITH BE FORCED TO SPEND THE REST OF HER LIFE AS A TWELVE-YEAR-OLD BOY?

CAN DMITRI AND MATHILDE LEAD THE CIRCUS TO VICTORY OVER CLAYTON JONES AND FRONTIER NEWS?

NOW THAT AMERICA KNOWS SUPERHEROES EXIST, WILL SADIE AND HUSSEIN UNLEASH THEIR POWERS IN PUBLIC?

IS THE WORLD READY FOR TWO FIRE BOYS?

THE ANSWERS TO THESE QUESTIONS AND MUCH MORE AWAIT IN ...

THE FINAL ADVENTURE OF FIRE BOY!

I wrote *Pants on Fire* in 2020 in the midst of lockdowns and a pandemic. Without the support of these talented and generous people, it would never have seen the light of day. My thanks go to:

My brilliant editor, Lena McCauley, and the whole team at Hachette.

Becky Bagnell, agent extraordinaire and part-time travel guide.

Samuel Perrett and his flame-tastic cover and designs.

The very talented Lucy Rogers who repeatedly spared my blushes with her yellow highlighter. Emma Roberts for proofreading a final copy.

Jenny Jones, my very good friend and wise advisor in all literary matters.

Jim Walton, Head of Clifton Preparatory School, for his support of my other career and the sabbatical which allowed me to write this novel.

Ash Bond, Helen Comerford, Elle Griffiths, Hilary Jelbert, Alison Powell and Bristol's Write Club for their wise counsel and feedback.

The booksellers, librarians, bloggers, teachers, parents and (especially) children who championed *Fire Boy* despite the illness, isolation, queues and cancellations which 2020 brought.

Claire, Max, Milo, Elaine and the O'Donovan clan for their cheer and enthusiasm.

Winnie and Rose for the walks.

Hannah, Conor and Ben: the one good thing to come out of lockdown was having you home again.

Mags, forever and always.

And finally, this book is dedicated to my sister, Beth, who welcomed me to New York so many moons ago and has always stood by me.

J. M. Joseph grew up on the East Coast of America surrounded by hills, forests and shopping malls. As soon as he was old enough, he crossed the ocean to Ireland, where he studied for four years, before settling in England. He now lives in Bristol with his wife, three children and two dogs.

FIRE BOY and **PANTS ON FIRE** are the first two books in his series about accidental superhero Aidan Sweeney.